VENGEANCE

IS MINE

VENGEANCE
IS MINE

———

Marie NDiaye

TRANSLATED FROM THE FRENCH
BY JORDAN STUMP

ALFRED A. KNOPF

NEW YORK

2023

THIS IS A BORZOI BOOK
PUBLISHED BY ALFRED A. KNOPF

www.aaknopf.com

A portion of this work originally appeared in *The Paris Review* (Spring 2023).

LIBRARY OF CONGRESS CATALOGING-IN-PUBLICATION DATA
Names: NDiaye, Marie, author. | Stump, Jordan, [date] translator.
Title: Vengeance is mine : a novel / Marie NDiaye ; translated from the French by Jordan Stump.
Other titles: Vengeance m'appartient. English
Description: First edition. | New York : Alfred A. Knopf, 2023. | "This is a Borzoi Book published by Alfred A. Knopf."
Identifiers: LCCN 2022060217 (print) | LCCN 2022060218 (ebook) | ISBN 9780593534243 (hardcover) | ISBN 9780593534250 (ebook)
Subjects: LCSH: Women lawyers—France—Fiction. | Murder—France—Fiction.
Classification: LCC PQ2674.D53 V4613 2023 (print) | LCC PQ2674.D53 (ebook) | DDC 843/.914—dc23/eng/20230531
LC record available at https://lccn.loc.gov/2022060217
LC ebook record available at https://lccn.loc.gov/2022060218

This is a work of fiction. Names, characters, places, and incidents either are the product of the author's imagination or are used fictitiously. Any resemblance to actual persons, living or dead, events, or locales is entirely coincidental.

Jacket image: (woman) by Marili Forastieri / Getty Images
Jacket design by Keenan

Manufactured in the United States of America
First American Edition

French lawyers are, in professional contexts, referred to by an honorific, of the same sort we might use to refer to a doctor or a professor. The title for a French lawyer is *Maître*—literally, "master." The central character of *Vengeance Is Mine* is referred to by a shortened form of that title throughout the novel. In Marie NDiaye's original she is known as "Me Susane"; to avoid confusion with the English word "me," I have chosen an alternate form of that abbreviation, and refer to her as "Me Susane" throughout, occasionally using the full form of the title for references to others.

All my thanks to Amanda Gerston, Eleanor Hardin, Kelly Kamrath, Marie NDiaye, and Annette Szlachta-McGinn for the invaluable help they've given me with this translation.

VENGEANCE

IS MINE

T HE MAN WHO TIMIDLY, almost fearfully entered her office on January 5, 2019, was, Me Susane realized at once, someone she'd met before, long before, in a place whose memory came back to her with such force and clarity that it felt like a sharp clout to her forehead.

Her head snapped back a little, momentarily preventing her from answering the uncomfortable mumble of her visitor's hello, and an awkwardness went on between them even after Me Susane sat down and greeted him warmly, with the cordial, reassuring smile she took care to show everyone who came to see her in her office.

Twice she distractedly rubbed her forehead, thinking she felt a dull ache there, then forgetting all about it.

When, that evening, sitting up in her bed, she would again raise a slow, heavy hand toward her brow and then stop herself, since it didn't actually hurt, she would suddenly remember her pain on seeing that man walk into her office, that slight, discreet man, as nondescript in his face as in his figure.

Which left her very surprised: Why had she felt anguish rather than joy?

Why, convinced that after thirty-two years she was seeing someone who had enraptured her, did she feel as if her life were in danger?

Me Susane listened as Gilles Principaux went on at length, several times thinking: I know you and I know your story, mingling her certainty that she'd once been very close to that man with what she knew from the papers of the sorrow that had come to him.

Not once, in that conversation, did he show any sign that he remembered meeting her, that that distant memory had even, perhaps, played some part in his decision to seek her out.

Because what high-profile cases did Me Susane have to her credit?

What, she wondered, could have motivated a well-to-do man, stricken but sane, to choose Me Susane for his wife's defense, if not, perhaps, a dim, superstitious allegiance to the luminous moments life had offered him?

But Principaux said nothing of the reasons, however confused, however foolish, for his choice.

He looked at Me Susane with a gaze at first evasive and then ever more assured as he answered her questions, and no matter how she tried Me Susane could not, in those eyes fixed on her face, make out any hint of an "I know you."

She couldn't very well ask him: Why did you come to me, I who am not a lawyer known throughout Bordeaux, particularly given the seriousness of the case? so she let him know that his wife, Marlyne Principaux, currently in custody, would have to formally accept Me Susane as her attorney.

Was that what she wanted?

"Of course it is," he answered, as if it went without saying, and suddenly there was something so brusque and so unlikable in his clenched features that for a moment Me Susane doubted she had before her the man she'd never forgotten.

"Maître Lasserre was my wife's lawyer before, but we don't like him, neither one of us," Principaux had told her when he came in. "So I want a new lawyer, for Marlyne's sake."

Just as Principaux was standing up to leave, she asked if he'd once lived in the Caudéran neighborhood.

"Yes," he said, "when I was young, why?"

He smiled at her then, and his whole face brightened joyously, childishly, now graced with a charm that Me Susane noted all the more keenly in that she'd found that same face, a minute earlier and to her acute disappointment, almost repellent.

But what was there to be disappointed about, whether Principaux was the one she remembered or had nothing to do with that afternoon?

Caught off guard, she answered that as a child she'd known a family in Caudéran.

She didn't need to hear him exclaim: There are lots of them! to realize the absurdity of her answer.

Yes, of course, many people lived in Caudéran.

Who, to her, was Gilles Principaux?

How to know, how to trust the thrilling, painful, disturbing intuition that he was once the teenager she'd fallen in love with for all time, long ago, in a Caudéran house that she couldn't possibly recognize today?

Mᵉ Susane found herself stumbling over her words.

"What was this family's name?" Principaux had asked with what seemed eager anticipation, as if already delighting in a connection he would surely find between himself and those people, and even, she thought, as if delighting in the prospect, if necessary, of inventing and substantiating a connection between himself and that family, simply to give Mᵉ Susane the pleasure of something shared, some bond amid everything else.

"I don't know, I mean I don't remember," Mᵉ Susane mumbled.

In the end she put on her lawyerly voice again and told him she'd be expecting Madame Principaux's letter appointing her to her defense.

She opened the door, stepped aside to let him out.

He leaned on the doorjamb and, in a weak, cavernous voice, whispered:

"Only you can save us."

Me Susane would later question her memory of that moment, uncertain whether he'd said "us" or "me."

He added something banal, something like:

"You'll get us out of this nightmare, won't you?"

At that Me Susane was more than a little taken aback.

Hoping to be rescued from the consequences of some terrible judicial mistake, some outrageous case of mistaken identity, that she would of course understand.

But in this case the nightmare hadn't arisen from some mix-up, some misunderstanding, it was this man's very life, and the acts that were ravaging that life had happened and couldn't be undone, since the dead were not going to extract themselves from his bad dream and be born a second time.

So, she wondered, did Principaux really want to be awakened?

Did he really believe that a bright and diaphanous morning would then dawn, and his children would come running to him, unhurt, joyous, and innocent?

Exactly what dream was he hoping, by way of Me Susane, to be freed from?

Freezing rain had put the tram out of service when she went home that night.

Had it been only the day before, feeling her shoes slip on the frozen pavement, her first thought would have been for Sharon.

I hope she managed to get the tram in time, Me Susane would have told herself, not liking to see her housekeeper ride off into the cold and the dark on her bicycle.

But this night she didn't think of Sharon, absorbed as she was in recalling every detail of Principaux's visit, already feeling anxious when she realized that some of his words hadn't indelibly fixed themselves in her memory (had he said "my wife" or "my spouse," had he used her first name or did Me Susane think she remembered it that way because she'd read the name Marlyne in the newspaper?), impatient to be back in her apartment so she could write down everything she had left in her head.

Who was Gilles Principaux to her?

And so, opening the door and finding every light ablaze in the hallway, the dining room, and the kitchen, she was briefly afraid, having forgotten that Sharon might still be there even with the tram shut down, despite Me Susane's many reminders that she was free to go home whenever she thought best, whether the work (of which there was in truth so little) was finished or not.

Me Susane had always said or suggested to Sharon that she would rather know Sharon was tranquilly looking after her children, helping them with their homework and judiciously thinking of their futures, than find her here at work late in the day.

It makes me uncomfortable, Me Susane didn't dare tell her, that you think it necessary to scour a bathtub I never soak in, to give a weekly washing to windows that are already clean and that I rarely look out of, and to scrub toilets I scrub every day so as to spare you any contact with my private functions, yes, Me Susane didn't dare tell her, it makes me very uncomfortable that you take my wish to employ someone to look after my interior so literally and that, in your uprightness and integrity, you somehow manage to spend hours putting the finishing touch on a job that out of modesty and consideration I've already seen to, it makes me uncomfortable, yes, Me Susane could not tell Sharon, she who until recently had never felt the need for a housekeeper, who even professed, against that need, an insurmountable prejudice.

Sharon, I employ you as an act of militancy, to help you and to further a cause I support, so you don't have to prove to me how scrupulous, honest, and irreproachable you are, as if you fear I might not be satisfied with your work, I always will be, Sharon, because in fact there's nothing I actually ask you to do, Me Susane did not say to her, again out of consideration, but of a different sort.

Her heart had not yet recovered from its surprise when Sharon came to meet her in the hallway.

Me Susane gave her the usual quick hug, she could feel her heart beating against the mute, serene, imperturbable breast that was Sharon's, Sharon who never physically showed any sign, ever strong, fatalistic, and upbeat, that her life might be harder than Me Susane's.

Sometimes Sharon seemed even to pity her.

Or so at least Me Susane liked to joke when she was invited to dinner and had, she told herself, to pay for her board with funny stories, since she never had guests.

She would cry out, heated and waggish, japing and pained:

"Can you imagine, my Sharon doesn't envy me at all, quite the contrary!"

And her friends would laugh, and then they would put on a

serious air as they tried to understand what could stop Sharon from grasping just how far Me Susane outstripped her when it came to happiness, what could stop Sharon from realizing she should wish she were Me Susane instead of who she was, an undocumented Mauritian blessed but also encumbered with two children of uncertain future and, Me Susane believed she had gleaned, a deeply depressed husband.

But wasn't all that just a jumble of speculations?

Because the face Sharon showed her was never anything but tranquil, and her heart beat softly, almost imperceptibly, when Me Susane embraced her, her own savage heart vainly trying to rile Sharon's, to fill it with her own fervor and revolt—but why?

Me Susane couldn't say.

"Sharon, you should have gone home, they've shut down the tram for the night."

Me Susane turned off the riotous lights beaming down from the ceiling.

Sharon, you don't have to turn on every light in the apartment, Me Susane didn't say either, because that mark of respect, that show of thoughtfulness you think you have to offer your employer when she comes home late and tired by dazzlingly illuminating her entrance, none of that suits my spirit of frugality, economy, and temperance in every act of daily life, no, Sharon, really, turn on only the lights you can't do without for your work, Me Susane would never, absolutely never, tell her.

She was so fond of Sharon that she found these little vexations not worth the risk of seeing even the shadow of a disappointment or an anxiety in the young woman's green-gray eyes.

Me Susane couldn't bear Sharon fearing anything that came from her.

I work for you, Sharon, I will never inflict the slightest unpleasantness on you, and I will never give you an order, said Me Susane mutely, hoping those charitable, uncontained, ardent thoughts would stream from her mind like eggs in a spawning bed, where Sharon's own thoughts, her unknowable emotions, would bond with Me Susane's silent declarations and she would perhaps feel hope, the result of an immaculate, unspoken fusion of fear and trust.

I'll never let you down, Sharon, believe in me, thought Me Susane, as hard as she could.

"I'm going to drive you home," she told Sharon.

Seeing her sudden unease, she added:

"I told you just now, the tram isn't running, there's ice on the tracks."

"That won't be possible, thanks, I have my bicycle, we can't fit it in the car," Sharon shot back.

Why did she often give Me Susane the feeling she wanted nothing to do with her outside the walls of this apartment?

Did she believe, did she fear (and why?), that Me Susane was hoping to become her friend?

Me Susane had no such ambition.

But she'd once happened onto Sharon and her children in a supermarket at the Lac shopping center, and she was stung to see Sharon very clearly pretending she hadn't spotted her.

Sharon, you're not placing yourself in any danger by consenting to recognize me, to say hello to me, to introduce me to your children, who are every bit your equals in beauty and grace, what harm could

I possibly do you, how could I ever seek to make you the victim of some evil spell?

I have no dark motive, Sharon, for employing you, it complicates my life, and I don't like to be served.

I'm simply trying, Sharon, to do good, in the way that I can.

Me Susane took off her ice-spangled jacket and hung it on the rack in the entryway before Sharon could take it from her.

Tiny, thin-faced, narrow-shouldered, slim-hipped, as if she'd made the decision to take up only the most minimal space in this world, the young woman looked up with her vague, gentle, tortured gaze at Me Susane, who was tall and wide, imposing and assured.

"I'll take you in the car," Me Susane said carefully, "and to-morrow morning you can come back in the tram to get your bicycle."

"No!" cried Sharon with a sort of fierce, unyielding anguish that shocked Me Susane. "That doesn't work for me," Sharon went on, slowly, "but thank you, thank you, thank you."

Me Susane raised her hand, conciliatory and humble, mortified.

Then, the incident forgotten (except by Me Susane, whose mind tended to wipe out her happiest memories and remember forever what there was no need to recall), Sharon put on an enthusiastic voice to describe everything she'd accomplished during her working hours in this apartment on the Rue Vital-Carles, an apartment certainly grand in its appointments (herringbone parquet floors, seventeenth-century fireplace, tall windows with little panes) but of middling surface area, forty

square meters in all likelihood carved from an imposing residence divided up long before for easier sale.

Me Susane knew there were no rational grounds for the
presence in her apartment of a vigorous, tireless, driven Sharon, determined to prove that her capacity for hard work was
being put to a useful and even necessary purpose.

Me Susane knew she didn't need Sharon's energy, youth, or
abilities, she knew full well that those virtues were wasted in
her apartment, where there was literally nothing to do.

But what choice did she have?

She was handling Sharon's case, her application for residency papers for her and her family.

"Well then, I'll see you tomorrow," she said. "Thanks, Sharon, and do be careful on your bicycle."

Suddenly she clasped Sharon's little hand, pulled it toward
her, and whispered:

"You know what, I'm going to be taking on a big case. A
woman who killed her three children, very young children, just
little kids, you understand."

Sharon snatched her hand away, a leap backward protecting
her from Me Susane, from her breath, her words, perhaps her
strange intensity.

"That's horrible," she mumbled in a cold, disgusted voice.

And it was as clear as if she'd closed her eyes and put her
hands over her ears: Oh, I don't want to hear another word!

She turned away, took her jacket from the coatrack, bent
down to pull on her fleece-lined boots.

Me Susane then noticed that the undersized collar of her

jacket, which was itself much too light for winter, did not cover Sharon's fine, golden, palpitating neck.

She hurried to her room and came back with an orange cashmere scarf.

Me Susane's mother had given it to her and she'd never worn it, too unsure of her own radiance to display that fire at her throat.

She wordlessly tied it around Sharon's neck.

I'm not saying anything, Sharon, because I don't want you to turn down my scarf, I don't want to argue about the possibility of your catching a chill tonight riding your bicycle all the way back to Lormont.

Sharon too kept her mouth shut, docile as an impotent child forced to endure the inexplicable violence of adults, and as she tied the two ends of the scarf over Sharon's nape Me Susane could or thought she could feel the young woman's delicate skeleton quivering in fright or repulsion beneath her fingers.

Only the day before, she would have been terribly hurt by that.

What is it in me, Sharon, that stops you from liking me even as I treat you with the greatest respect and see to your case out of the goodness of my heart, since I won't be charging you for my work? Does it never occur to you, Sharon, that I could have refused to take your case without payment, which would have left you helpless and alone, you don't have any money, I wouldn't have dealt with your problem, I never would have gotten involved in your life? How, Sharon, can you not understand the way things are? How can you be so devoted and so fickle, so meticulous and so ungrateful, so sensitive in general and so brusque with me? Am I not, Sharon, a woman exactly like you?

Yes, only the day before, she would have been so shaken by

Sharon's behavior that sadness and rancor would have filled her as she ate the dinner her employee had made.

She would have dined on spitefulness, on sorrow, a dish of tears, hers, shameful and humiliating, unable to enjoy the fare Sharon had so exquisitely prepared, too overcome even to console herself with the thought that Sharon could never have cooked like this for someone she hated, which could only mean that Sharon didn't hate her, and Me Susane was being ridiculous and oversensitive.

But that evening she calmly let Sharon set off for home in her furtive, tense, hostile way, as if some grave, unspoken conflict had erupted between them.

She closed the door, and immediately her thoughts wandered far away from Sharon.

She reheated the fried rice, the shrimp with ginger, the sautéed pork with garlic, the very tender carrots.

And although, her thoughts fixed on Principaux, she'd forgotten Sharon, or rather relegated her to a corner of her mind where nothing carried any weight, she enjoyed Sharon's dinner as she rarely had before.

Nonetheless, though she'd always been a sound sleeper, she was awakened that night by a question that wouldn't leave her alone: Why was Principaux turning to her, how did he know her?

Should she interpret that choice as Principaux's desire to give his wife the best possible defense, or on the contrary was it his perfidious intention that her defense not be all that good?

Because Me Susane had opened her office only the year before, and she'd had just a handful of clients, cases of no interest.

If she were Principaux, she told herself, she would have gone to see Maître *** or Maître ***, whose successes in difficult cases were known far and wide, certainly not the obscure Me Susane who, though aged forty-two, could easily be thought a novice.

Any big-name lawyer would have leapt at the chance to defend Marlyne Principaux, whereas for Me Susane it should have been nothing more than a dream.

Who was Gilles Principaux to her?

Who was Me Susane to Principaux?

Did they have the same memories, she wondered, or were neither he nor she the person they thought they remembered?

A bit before dawn, just as she was drifting off for scarcely two hours more, she had an image of the slight Sharon pedaling through the icy streets toward Lormont, hurrying back to a household of which she was, as Me Susane understood it, the hub.

Then she couldn't help but see Sharon fallen to the ground, blood flowing from her head and soaking the orange scarf that would attest to Me Susane's brutality—because wouldn't any normally solicitous employer have insisted on keeping her housekeeper safe, would anyone think it enough to tie a scarf around her neck before turning her out onto the treacherous streets?

Me Susane tossed back and forth a few times in her bed.

She laid out her defense: I wanted her to stay, I repeated the offer, she refused with that way of hers, as if she'd rather die than . . .

No one would believe such a story, she'd only be digging herself in deeper, thought Me Susane, with a sadness and a sense of incompetence that colored her dreams until morning.

And at eight o'clock she was out again, again in the dark, walking against the frigid wind to the parking lot under the Allées de Tourny.

Me Susane found a certain vain delight in convincing her friends that she had no interest in owning a high-status vehicle, that she was perfectly happy driving a battered twenty-year-old Twingo, that she was proud to display her indifference to such conventional notions of social standing.

Me Susane wasn't unhappy to let her friends see her that way: bohemian, fanciful, independent—hoping deep inside that in time their image of her would shape her, would force her to live up to it, and she would actually become a woman of discreetly eccentric charm.

That, Me Susane knew, was pure fantasy.

She yearned to be rich enough to buy a big, beautiful, sumptuous car.

She was thoroughly sick of her dear old Twingo, and sensed that her parents could scarcely bear the thought of her still driving that car when they wanted to see her prospering, since that was the picture she gave them when she told them of her work and her life (oh, she loved them so!).

Her parents lived in La Réole, where Me Susane had spent her childhood and adolescence.

If Monsieur Susane, a city employee, had looked favorably

on his daughter going to college, it was because he thought it went without saying that she would go on to work for the city as well, and his pleasure, his quiet boast, suited to the modest man he was, was to say:

"One day she'll be my boss, she'll be giving me orders!"

Me Susane had always thought that her gentle, amiable father could imagine no more glorious success than a daughter overseeing men such as him.

Proud and humble, he liked to say:

"She's got more on the ball than we do."

A vaster ambition, vaguer, more torn, had led Madame Susane to follow her daughter's studies as closely as she could, encouraging her, spurring her on even as Me Susane, become a young woman, was tormented by her own tendency to drive herself too hard, she didn't need to be encouraged or spurred on, she would rather have been quieted, restrained in her hunger for work, and Madame Susane's exhortations, at once loving, anxious, and haphazard (because she couldn't grasp what her daughter was studying, she could only give it an occasional intimidated glance), often brought her to the brink of nervous exhaustion.

And then, with sorrow and terror, Me Susane had taken to thinking that only a slender thread (her boundless love for them? her pride?) prevented her from falling into what her mother most dreaded and so heavy-handedly endeavored to protect her from: the abandonment of lofty aspirations, the retreat to a mediocre way of life, comfortable, befitting her rank.

She loved them so!

And how it hurt to love them, sometimes!

They understood her so well, but so little in the way Me Susane wanted to be understood—with her ordinary weaknesses, which they didn't see, with her fears, which they couldn't imagine!

She loved them so, and sometimes it so hurt her to love them that she wished, tormented, wretched, and ashamed, that they would just disappear!

Because she loved them so, and what else could she do but lie to them, or at least give them a glittering version of her existence, of the world in general, to shield them from the painful truth?

But who were they, Me Susane asked herself, to be spared the painful truth, to be protected from their own moments of ignorance, passivity, and religious complacency in the face of life's hard realities?

Sometimes she resented them for being the kind of people who needed to be spared things, to be sheltered from unhappiness simply because they were good-hearted and emotional.

Give safe harbor to my troubled heart, console me, hear my pleas, see the signs of a sorrow that's devouring me, that I myself can't define—rescue me as all vigilant parents do!

All the thoughtful parents Me Susane knew looked on their adult children with a gaze free of illusions.

They walked beside them, pragmatic and tireless, one arm always at the ready in case of a stumble, all advice sealed away, and in their relationships there was no room for disappointment, felt or expressed.

Whereas Me Susane never forgot that any remark carelessly let slip before her parents, a complaint, an ordinary regret, could transform their forthright, unguarded, smiling faces into masks of anxiety.

It was so unreasonable that it annoyed her, and immediately after filled her with pity.

She reassured them, all the while thinking: When will it be your turn to reassure me? Is it right to virtually forbid me to confess my failings to you?

But they loved her so, she knew!

And in their immeasurable love, did they sometimes wish for a respite from that love, did they sometimes wish Me Susane would disappear?

She would have understood perfectly, she told herself.

That morning, that cold, sharp morning, as she drove toward La Réole on a highway packed with automobiles far more powerful than hers, making her feel she had to squeeze into the right-hand lane so they could deploy their self-proclaimed eminence, she thought once again that, were it not for the car, which made it impossible to lie, Monsieur and Madame Susane would have been entirely capable of convincing themselves that their daughter had a flourishing career.

She could tell them whatever she liked.

She'd worked for a big law firm in Bordeaux, and then, two years ago, she decided to open her own, to take the plunge, as her parents said, not knowing what to think of such a venture.

What they trusted was the car, Me Susane knew.

For them makes and models were the indisputable measure of failure or success.

They were right, they were right!

Me Susane was ashamed to want a new car.

But she thought it might give her self-esteem a boost, since her parents would love her even more.

Although they knew nothing, understood nothing, they could see it clearly through the fog of their thoughts: Me Susane's practice was not thriving.

Wasn't it only natural that, disappointed as they were the only parents who dared to be, they redoubled their affection for Me Susane and looked with distress on her aged Twingo, like unclean clothes, mused Me Susane, a sign that their daughter was not leading her life with the rigor they'd taught her?

She parked by the river, far enough from their house that they wouldn't see her car from their windows (they'd been known to forget the subject when it wasn't there before their eyes), then climbed the exhausting staircase that led to the old town.

She walked down dark, narrow streets.

The gray dawn was little different from night.

Her parents' house was the last in an impasse closed off by a high cinder block wall—that dear house, that matchless house of her radiant childhood!

It was here that the notion of a perfect home was born in Me Susane's understanding, then spread all through her being as she grew up in this place, even if, as she'd slowly come to realize, there was nothing enviable about it, it was cramped, dark, damp.

Until the day she went with her mother to a certain house in Caudéran, her La Réole home seemed to her an enchanted abode.

She loved it no less on her return from Caudéran, but she'd noticed, her eyes abruptly opened, that other houses were enchanted abodes, and enchanted far more intensely.

Who was Gilles Principaux to her?

How could Principaux have come from a splendorous Caudéran and ended up amid the horrific scene she'd read about in the papers?

What if, she suddenly wondered as she knocked at her parents' door, what if the horror was born of the splendor, and suppose he'd chosen exactly the wife who would punish him for growing up in the word of fairies?

But was she, Me Susane, thinking of the right person? *Who was Gilles Principaux in her life?*

That was more or less the question she put to Madame Susane once the coffee was drunk and she'd assured her parents, surprised at her visit, that everything was going swimmingly in her life.

In the little kitchen that looked onto the impasse, dimly lit by the ceiling lamp of green opaline and forged iron, she felt tranquil and in command of herself as she always did when she crossed this house's threshold, in spite of the usual flash of apprehension she'd seen in her parents' eyes when she came in.

They seemed to be saying to her, embarrassed and on edge: Everything's fine for us, we've got no worries, we don't want you making any unpleasant announcements, although it's our job to welcome you, to hear bad news, but that's not what we want, we struggle for all we're worth to fend that off, that's why we had only one child, you, whom we love but whom we sometimes wish we could never hear from, for fear that any news might be bad news. Which makes us sometimes envy a certain sort of tranquility: the tranquility of loving couples who were wise enough not to have (or who wisely resigned themselves to not having) a child, who can always be a source of bad news or disappointments, even monstrousness and tales of horrific scenes, and that child, now suddenly a stranger, that fruit of our desire and our pride, inspires in us a bitter thought: Nothing was forcing us, we were weak and vain and now here is that woman, our daughter, showing up at dawn on a winter day to tell us something that might overturn our serenity forever.

Me Susane would remember saying to her mother, pretending not to notice that the latter seemed to be putting up her guard, something like (her tone friendly, her voice carefree):

"Mama, do you remember, I once came with you to a house in Caudéran where you were working, it was a Wednesday, so no school, and there was nothing else you could do but bring me along, I must have been ten years old, I imagine."

"I don't know, I don't remember," Madame Susane answered slowly.

She put on the theatrical expression of raising her eyes toward the opaline ceiling lamp and its cold off-green light, as if summoning her memories, lips pinched to signify effort and uncertainty.

"I worked in a lot of houses in Bordeaux, you know, I can't keep them all straight."

"Yes, of course," said Me Susane. "The people who lived there might have been called Principaux."

"Principaux like that woman who . . . ?"

"Yes. I was just wondering, just curious, if it was the same family . . ."

Never had Me Susane awaited an answer with such hope and trepidation, not knowing what it was she wanted to hear.

But she must have known deep inside, because she was disappointed when Madame Susane, categorical, immoveable, immune to any sort of pressure, assured her she had no memory of working for a Principaux.

"Maybe," Me Susane dared to say, "maybe you've forgotten the names of some of the people you worked for?"

"Well, of course I have," grumbled Madame Susane, "how do you expect me to remember them, and why would I bother, you think they remember *my* name?"

"So you might have worked in the Principaux house in Caudéran and not remember?"

To her deep dismay Me Susane heard herself almost pleading.

She was trying to tease out a truth that matched what she'd secretly come looking for, not knowing if that truth would be good for her.

And Madame Susane was deliberately resisting, determined not to remember the name Principaux, if that was the name.

But to what extent was she not remembering only because she sensed that her daughter desperately wanted her to?

Me Susane wasn't convinced.

So she let herself go, she dropped her playacting voice, her ostentatiously casual voice, she let the tone of her story match the agitation that was suddenly making her sweat and tremble beneath the opaline ceiling light, leaving her breathless as a cornered doe.

And yet her story was a joyous one, she thought.

She found herself gasping, at once on fire and numb with cold, as if there were anything at all hard about recounting the happiest moment of her life.

Madame Susane eyed her intently, eager and anxious, possibly approving all the same.

She first interrupted Me Susane to exclaim:

"It's true, yes, that house was marvelous!"

And then again, almost shouting:

"I loved those people, they were fantastic."

And she added, slightly offending her linguistic modesty, and so with a touch of defiance, courage, insistence on honesty:

"They were kindness itself, weren't they?"

Me Susane found herself quibbling (but what a lot she'd already gotten from an ordinarily so reserved Madame Susane!).

She wanted it to be clear that the family in Caudéran who might not have borne the name Principaux was probably not so much kind as bewitching.

"But the result is the same," said Madame Susane, "they were kind, they were admirable, and they were very, very friendly, right?"

"They put a spell on us," said Me Susane with a mirthless little laugh.

That was how she concluded her story.

Smiling to herself, her mother said softly:

"I entered that house like it was the milky wood."

"What on earth are you talking about?" snapped Monsieur Susane.

He hadn't yet spoken a word.

Me Susane remembered: he didn't like mysteries, he found strangeness personally humiliating.

He disapproved of any fondness for life's paradoxes, odd co-incidences, conjectures, and daydreams.

He was gentle and good all the same, and Me Susane, that man's only child, could not recall one time when he'd scorned or chided her for no reason.

How she loved him!

And it was because she so loved her down-to-earth father that she had to smile when Madame Susane said "milky wood," hoping her indulgent little smile would reassure her father that she was on his side, where reason ruled.

But, astonished, she said to herself: That's just what it was, it was the milky wood, it was the place where pure and simple joy subjugated us as if by enchantment.

"Would you," she asked Madame Susane, "be able to find that house in Caudéran again? Do you remember the address?"

Her mother regretfully shook her head.

"I only went there once, you know."

Then, speaking to Monsieur Susane with an air of modest defiance, she told him about that winter day some thirty years before, when she'd gone to do ironing for those people in Caudéran whose name she couldn't remember, about whom she'd forgotten everything, what their house looked like, their faces, their words, their dress, but never the kindly welcome they'd given her (because, in truth, she'd felt like an honored guest in the home of that couple whose usual housekeeper she was replacing just for the day).

She'd ironed the laundry in the kitchen, their clothes were soft and elegant, scarcely wrinkled, as if those very clothes meant to treat her kindly, and the kitchen seemed a gracious counterpart of her own, not because they looked the same but because the room, also endowed with good-hearted intentions, had greeted her warmly and thoughtfully, and said to her: You're at home here, and Madame Susane had acquiesced without the shadow of a snide second thought, she who, working for others since she was a teenager, regularly spoke of her employers with bitter derision.

That was almost a mania of hers, she admitted, because she stopped making any distinction between the nice ones and the mean ones, she stirred them up all together in the same big pot of caustic mockery.

"But not those people, never," Madame Susane affirmed, staring at her husband as if to stop him from contradicting her.

The woman in Caudéran had offered her a cup of coffee, and orange juice for the little girl who was with her. The man had come out of his study to say hello and welcome her to the house.

Madame Susane confessed that she would have felt uncomfortable had she not immediately realized that that couple's cordiality was of a piece with their nature, that they weren't feigning delight at her presence but were truly delighted, and would be for as long as they'd be uniting that presence with theirs in this house, like good dogs, Madame Susane explained in all seriousness, who are overjoyed to see people even if they'll forget all about the visitors once they've gone on their way.

That's how it was, yes, said Madame Susane in conclusion, her ephemeral employers in Caudéran had very simply displayed a pleasure at having her with them, such as she'd never felt in any other house.

Add to that their generosity: they paid her twice what she usually asked, without a word about it, without telling her they were doing it, in a spirit as open and, almost, as innocent as the spirit that moved the Caudéran woman to ask, looking into the kitchen several times over the afternoon, if "everything was fine, really," her voice warm and gentle, bright and attentive.

"So I hope you understand," Madame Susane said to her husband with some sharpness, "I hope you understand now why I remember that house like a supernatural place?"

"Yes," mumbled Monsieur Susane.

"Like a wonderland?"

He nodded, though he wasn't pleased.

"So I have every right to say 'milky wood,' what does it matter to you?"

"It matters," Monsieur Susane said coolly, "because I don't like those words, they're deceptive."

Me Susane stood up, rinsed her cup in the sink.

Now she was eager to be off, not having gotten an answer to the question that had brought her here:

Was there any connection between Principaux and the milky wood of Caudéran?

Not to mention that she could feel an unwonted irritability vibrating between her parents, and she blamed herself for bringing it on.

But before she could tell them she was starting back for

Bordeaux, Monsieur Susane came to her, put a gentle, loving hand on her hair, just above her ear.

"My little girl," he murmured with a smile, "you work too hard, you're already wanting to get away, I can see it."

She protested feebly, even as she intimated that she had a stack of files waiting.

In truth there were virtually none: two amicable divorces, a change of name, and the residency permit request for Sharon's family.

Her poor parents, how she misled them!

"I don't quite understand," Monsieur Susane said in a thick voice, "what happened in that bedroom in Caudéran. What exactly did that guy do?"

"But, Papa, I just told you!" Me Susane objected.

She was so shocked that her elbow hit the sink and made her drop her cup, which shattered on the floor.

Glad of the diversion, Me Susane set about picking up the pieces.

Still crouching, her face bent over the floor tiles, she went on:

"I don't understand your question, Papa. I just told you all about that afternoon, I didn't leave out a single detail if it had any importance and any interest in the context of my story, if it had some eloquent meaning, and I also, I think, suggested that the few hours I spent with that young man (that's how I saw him, I was all of ten years old, he can't have been more than fourteen or fifteen) are among those I recall today with delight, and with nostalgia as well, since, it's true, I might not have told you this, I never again found in any boy, any man, any living being, the strange charm that in a way fated me to adore him."

"But what did he do?" asked Monsieur Susane in a pained voice.

"Nothing, Papa! Don't you understand? Absolutely nothing of the sort you mean!"

What had he done? she asked herself on the drive back, her hands trembling slightly on the wheel.

What had that boy who might have been Gilles Principaux done in that room, his room, which he'd so gallantly invited her to enter?

He'd noticed that little girl sitting close by her mother as she ironed the laundry in the kitchen.

He'd probably said to her something like:

"You must be bored sitting there doing nothing, come with me, I'll show you my room."

She'd followed him, at once dazed at the honor and anxious to prove herself worthy of that distinction, after a glance at her mother, who, Me Susane thought she remembered, gave her a big, benevolent smile: "Go on, my girl, go have some fun!"

Her already-subjugated mother, happy and grateful, her trusting mother, ambitious for Me Susane, wanting her daughter to show she was curious and intrepid, to meet people, people different from them (Monsieur and Madame Susane, perfectly happy with what they were, wanting nothing more than what they had), and aiming to lift her daughter high above her own station, her naïve, madly loving mother, at once happy with her lot and yearning to see Me Susane look with horror, for her own sake, on that lot!

Go on (do as he says), follow that boy who's better schooled than your father and I will ever be, and lay your hungry eyes on the walls of that room, which must surely be hung with interesting art- work, on the shelves no doubt stocked with the books you don't find at home, go on (do as he says, be polite) and begin your own fruitful education, go, go, run away from us, escape our humble influence (do as he says, be polite)!

Because that's how her mother was: anxious to see M^e Su- sane rise, and aware of her own deficiencies, though feeling no pointless shame about them.

The teenager who might have been Gilles Principaux showed Me Susane his fossil collection, played her a Dire Straits record.

He had her sit down beside him on the couch that took up one corner of the room, a corner that seemed very distant from the bed, from the armoire, like a little parlor removed from the room's practical functions, which she thought the last word in elegance.

In a voice at once detached and honeyed, blasé and courtly, he asked what she thought of it all: the fossils, the music, the house's general atmosphere.

And Me Susane, who had never been asked to analyze and to criticize what she was seeing, after a few seconds of terror, boldly spoke up, disclosing, in a tone at first fearful and then ever more confident, her delight, her enthusiasm, admitting that she was thoroughly in love with this room and this house and this family and trying, with her ten-year-old's words and tastes, to make those feelings clear.

As it turned out, the boy wasn't easy to please.

He rebuked her for her slightest grammatical slips.

He very quietly clucked his tongue when she digressed or showed some sort of inelegance, inciting her, even obliging her (she was so eager to please him!) to immediately understand what he expected of her, as Me Susane had seen her parents do training Bouly, her childhood dog.

She pulled out all the most insightful, the cleverest, the most beguiling, the most artful things her mind contained.

The boy seemed happy with her, he stroked her hair, which at the time was long and silky.

He complimented her, flattered her, and he also graded her, with a score whose number Me Susane couldn't remember.

Did he say to her: You're a good little pupil, I'm very pleased with you?

Me Susane wasn't sure.

She might have made up those words that night in her bed, still stirred and quivering with the almost unendurable emotions of the afternoon, which had ended in a torrent of speech from her.

Because she couldn't stop talking to the boy who, she thought she remembered, simply listened, sometimes spurring her on with a word, a question, no doubt amused and assuredly proud that with so little work he had led this girl to know herself or to glimpse what she might become.

"It's all thanks to him," Me Susane had just confided to her parents, "that I'm a lawyer today."

And then her face grew hot under the effect of a slight unease, as if, certain she was being sincere, she discovered as she spoke that she wasn't entirely, though she didn't see in what way she was being insincere, not to mention why, since she was opening her heart to her parents for the very first time.

But what did he do to you in that bedroom?

How offensive she found Monsieur Susane's question!

She was choking with anger, paying little attention to the road.

So her father had understood nothing, as always, even though he swore he loved her (even though he did love her, and wasn't that worse?).

What he did to me, Me Susane was merciful enough not to say, was what parents are supposed to do for their children, he made me understand the pleasures I enjoyed and the talent I probably had for arguing and expounding and his hands ran over my hair, my cheeks, my neck, his hands were pleased with me, they cuddled me like happy parents do, or the way you used to reward Bouly when he'd done well in his training.

Nothing more than that!

And Bouly loved you for as long as he lived, didn't he?

To Bouly, didn't all the happiness in this world depend on you two?

Me Susane pulled off the highway at a service area.

Her thoughts were becoming muddled, she was pleading the case incompetently, but who was she actually pleading for?

For Principaux?

For the Caudéran boy who was possibly not Principaux?

Or for herself, in her insistence on seeing that long-ago afternoon as the happiest and rightest of her existence?

She was prepared to mount an ardent defense of the boy before her parents and her own inevitably nebulous memories.

She had far more faith in the opinion she'd forged of that boy thirty years before than in the picture she had of him now, influenced and transformed by the way people think nowadays.

Her father, Monsieur Susane . . .

In the gas station restroom she ran cold water over her shaking hands, forced a smile in the mirror.

Her father, Monsieur Susane, no doubt jealous of the Caudéran boy, of what that boy had transfigured in her, had tried, awkwardly (because deep down he was a kindly man) to sully that memory, at least a little.

What of it?

Monsieur Susane had his reasons, who cares?

She loved him, and at the same time she passionately loved her memory of Caudéran, of that boy who'd initiated her, illuminated her!

She understood them all, her dubious, untrusting father, her blind, visionary mother, and that teenaged boy, playful, educational, charmed almost in spite of himself and to his own surprise.

Because she'd amazed him and won him over, she'd offered up a virtuoso soliloquy, passionate, spirited (on what subject she couldn't recall), and that older boy had recognized her talent, had perhaps even spoken this sentence: You're good at that, way to go! while she went on talking until she ran out of breath, at once intoxicated and anxious, assured and panicked—although she was in no danger, Me Susane told herself as she got back into her car, of having her throat slit when her prolixity began to falter.

No, the boy would not have gone that far.

Just now, talking to her parents, she'd joked:

"It's not like I was the young maiden facing the cruel sultan!"

Back in Bordeaux, rather than make straight for the office she turned off toward the Caudéran neighborhood, with its mausoleal houses, its manicured park.

It was still so cold and gray that the few passersby, their faces masked by scarves, upturned collars, knit caps, or fur hats, seemed to move through the streets like shadows on a cemetery's walkways.

She drove slowly, studying every façade, trying to remember the house she and her mother had walked into three decades before.

She vaguely pictured brick corner details, maybe discreet columns, several stone balconies.

Nothing was certain.

She would, she thought, have recognized the kitchen, the boy's bedroom, its position relative to the kitchen—but of the house, its dimensions compared to the others, she had no recollection.

That infuriated her, left her as displeased with herself as

if this were all a failure not of her memory but of her intelligence, of her capacity for dealing with any situation that really mattered to her.

She cruised the streets longer than necessary.

She admitted to herself that she was looking for Principaux, even as she knew he no longer lived around there.

But he could have decided, couldn't he, to pay a call on his parents that cold, dreary morning, she would see him open a door or ring a bell and then she would know that he was one and the same with the teenaged boy permanently lodged in her soul—*an encysted tumor?*

Me Susane vigorously shook her head, answering herself with a sort of indignation.

She stopped in a parking lot, called her mother.

"What that boy is, Mama, is the encystment of pure joy!"

"Yes," said Madame Susane.

"Mama, what did the house look like?"

Madame Susane took a moment to think:

"I believe it was a Moorish-style villa," she finally said, tentative, almost questioning.

"Moorish, really, you think so? I don't know of any in that neighborhood."

"Yes," Madame Susane hurried to answer, "that's because they demolished it not long ago, I read about it in the newspaper."

"Oh, but you're mixing up two different things!"

Me Susane tried to conceal the depth of her disappointment.

"You're thinking of the Villa Mauresque, that was a house in Pessac, Mama, not Caudéran, it was abandoned, and yes, it was torn down a few years ago. That's nothing to do with what I'm talking about, with the house of those people who . . ."

Madame Susane interrupted her:

"In any case that's how I see it in my memory, an Oriental-style house, strange, magnificent, completely different from the others, that's why I said Moorish, I could just as well have said—"

She broke off, and the line went dead.

Dumbstruck, Mᵉ Susane could only conclude that her mother had hung up on her.

She was about to call her back when Madame Susane sent her a text:

"I'll stop there, your father's tired of all this, I don't want to quarrel with him, you understand. What he says about you is this: Either she talks and tells the truth (he's thinking of that afternoon) or she keeps quiet and we forget the whole thing, no more nonsense. You know him, he can be blunt, sometimes too blunt. I myself believe what you say, the boy instructed you, opened you up, educated you as we couldn't. Your father doesn't want to understand that, it's only normal. He's a practical man, he only sees bodies, breaths, turpitudes, he doesn't trust men (males), he doesn't like them, sometimes he'd like to kill them all (ha ha!), even the ones who are just fifteen years old, poor boys! Don't answer me, I'd rather your father not know (that you're answering me, the little ping of the phone) since just now I'm writing in secret. Adieu, my beloved daughter."

Mᵉ Susane had often heard old people in this region use "adieu" for "au revoir," even for "bonjour," but she'd never heard it from her mother.

That worried her, and then she was annoyed at being worried, and resentful toward Madame Susane for creating mysteries and toward Monsieur Susane for adamantly, closed-mindedly opposing those mysteries.

Yes, she loved them so much that she sometimes wished she could never again have anything to do with them, her beloved, exhausting parents, her unperceptive parents (and how easy it was, she thought, to be pure like them when you're protected from repellent truths!).

Back when she worked as an associate in the office on the Place de Tourny, Me Susane could never talk to them about certain cases she thought tremendously interesting.

"Stop!" they would cry, in a tone at once playful and firm, "it's too awful, we don't want to hear about it!"

And then she felt vaguely dirty, indecent, amoral, because she was captivated by that sort of thing.

Their unyielding refusal to learn what the simplicity of their life and thoughts kept them from knowing about the behavior of their contemporaries forbade her to feel any perfectly legitimate curiosity.

Sometimes she was dimly ashamed of her interest in her clients' stories and lives.

And she was angry at her parents for that shame—who were they to . . .

"All right, then, Mama dearest, adieu!" Me Susane murmured to herself.

She added her parents' number to the blocked-call list.

Then she drove off, doing her best to feel unburdened, but

filled with a sadness, a melancholy that she blamed on the cold, livid sky and her old car with its defective heater.

Her blue-tinged fingers feebly clutched the wheel.

She was shivering in her coat, in the many folds of the scarf around her neck, a gray scarf she thought of as elegant, in a discreet, refined style that her mother should have known was the sort of thing she liked, or at least what she would allow herself to wear (and was that so different?).

Why, the Christmas before, had Madame Susane given her that pumpkin-colored wool scarf?

Neither Me Susane nor her parents ever wore such colors.

Is that how Madame Susane dreamt of seeing her daughter, exuberant and whimsical, with the extravagance of a flame on her collar like a free spirit's profession of faith?

Telling herself how glad she was that she'd forced Sharon to go home under the protection of that orange scarf, hoping Sharon wouldn't feel obliged to bring it back to her but feeling no confidence in that hope, Me Susane, gripped by an amorphous intuition, decided to stop by her apartment before going on to the office.

Sharon wasn't there, which was not how it should have been.

Me Susane ate lunch (finished the excellent leftovers of the dinner Sharon had cooked), waited until two o'clock, then finally went on her way.

She'd called Sharon in vain, going straight to voice mail every time.

She was almost at her office door when an apprehension changed her mind.

She got back into her car and ordered the GPS to guide her to Sharon's address in Lormont.

Bordeaux was engulfed in fog, still as icy as ever, and Me Susane felt as if she were groping her way as she drove, inching along, seeing little in her headlights' faint glow but propelled by the insistent certainty that she had to go looking for Sharon where she lived, a place she'd never been before, where she'd never once thought of going, actively engaged though she was in Sharon's affairs: that residency permit for her and her husband and children.

A friend of Me Susane's, she couldn't even remember which one, having so many friends of no consequence, had, at dinner one night, tossed out the question:

"Would anyone be interested in my housekeeper? She's from Mauritius, no papers, but apart from that irreproachable."

And Me Susane had spoken up at once, not because she wanted a housekeeper or actually had the means to pay for it legally, but because she found the friend's cavalier attitude shameful.

"You should care a little about her situation," she'd told him, "and especially if you think highly of her, you can't just be satisfied with giving her work and not trying to help her."

"Well, what do you want me to do?" that vague friend had answered. "You deal with her, you're the only one here who can manage it properly."

And so Sharon had come into Me Susane's life and her work, even if she wasn't entirely sure Sharon realized it.

Several times already she'd asked Sharon for a copy of her marriage certificate, explaining that she needed it to get the process started with the authorities, also telling her that if Sharon didn't have or couldn't find that certificate she had to tell her right away so that she, Me Susane, could put the file together differently.

Sharon promised to bring her the paper.

The look on her face was troubled and hurt, as if Me Susane were trying to get her hands on something intensely personal, something Sharon could only surrender to her with deep regret.

It had been six weeks now.

Me Susane was still waiting for the certificate.

She'd brought it up with Sharon again, gently, but more than once.

Every time, Sharon put on her wounded, brave, distant air, assuring her almost inaudibly that she hadn't forgotten, and every time, Me Susane found herself abashed, absurdly embarrassed, as if she'd done some sort of violence to Sharon's wholesome morality.

In the end she gave up telling her over and over: Sharon, if you don't have the paper, just let me know, it's not that serious, I can manage, because when she did Sharon made it clear that she was offended (because presumably Me Susane suspected she was unmarried, and on that basis judged her harshly?).

Sharon, this is childish, Me Susane couldn't say to her, I don't care in the least whether you are or are not married to the father of your children or the man who followed you to France and you call their father, just tell me, Sharon, what your situation is, and I'll do what has to be done to best serve you. I took a vow, Sharon, to judge no one, especially not a woman like you, not ever.

Me Susane forced herself not to speak those words, sensing that Sharon would make them mean the opposite, that she would convince herself Me Susane was proclaiming her broadness of mind only to conceal her skepticism (regarding the truth of Sharon's marital status).

It took her longer than she expected to find the building.

It was an old house converted into apartments, built just by a busy street.

Me Susane left her car on the narrow sidewalk, not feeling up to the search for a proper parking spot in this unknown neighborhood.

Seeing neither a bell nor an intercom, she pushed on the half-open door and found herself in a hallway crammed with overflowing trash cans, old bicycles, strollers, the floor littered with flyers.

The cold and the damp bleakly underscored that amalgam of rancid odors.

So every day Sharon, a tidy young woman, her skin glowing with health, walked through this stinking, unwholesome hallway, as did her two children, and their fine, smooth faces, exquisite and perfect, passed through this foul air, were begrimed by invisible particles from this noxious atmosphere!

Me Susane felt an excessive, improper indignation swelling inside her.

She forbade herself to devote one more thought to those kids, whose lot had no reason to matter to her any more than many others'.

But she'd felt so hurt, to her own surprise, when Sharon pretended not to see her in the supermarket aisle she was walking down with her children that Me Susane found herself thinking she would be deeply honored were she finally permitted to make the acquaintance of the little girl and boy with their perfectly pure features.

And that hope made her feel, for those nippers (as she called them to herself, an old-fashioned, affectionate word freely used by Monsieur et Madame Susane: "Look, our nipper's here!" Monsieur Susane liked to call out when she came to visit), a protectiveness heavily marked by concern.

Uncertain what to do, she decided to climb the stairs rather than first knock at the doors on the ground floor, believing she recalled Sharon speaking of an arduous staircase she had to scale when she came home laden with shopping bags—one of the few mentions, perhaps the only one, that Sharon had made of her life in Lormont.

No, there had been another one, though Me Susane couldn't remember what it was (something to do with her husband, her children, her apartment, no telling! She'd been quietly shocked by it all the same, but on what grounds?).

The staircase was narrow and steep.

It was designed to lead to the bedrooms of this onetime private house, not to be climbed to an apartment by the mother of several children, a mother on whom, Me Susane had grasped, the survival of her family wholly depended.

She gave a tentative knock on the door nearest the staircase.

Everything appalled her, disgusted her, but nothing surprised her.

Who dares, probably asking a great deal of money, to rent

out such a place, peeling walls, ancient electrical sockets, the transom walled up? she thought, in a rush of automatic but no less sincere rage.

A long moment went by, and then the door cracked open to reveal the anxious, untrusting face of a man who looked like Sharon and her magnificent children: golden brown, delicate, with sensitive, quivering eyelids.

"I'm Me Susane, Sharon's employer."

She was smiling too brightly, trying to reassure him.

He murmured something she didn't understand, and then, forcing himself to match her broad smile, he opened the door wider, with dread in his beautiful eyes.

My God, what are you doing here? What horrible news is your smile hiding?

"Everything's fine," Me Susane hurried to say, "I was just wondering if Sharon might have stayed home today, what with this cold . . ."

He paused to think, quickly and desperately reckoning (oh, how deeply Me Susane pitied him!) what he could say to her that wouldn't put them all at risk.

"She—she went off to work," he stammered, "yes, I think, yes."

Then, in a more confident tone:

"Come in, madame, come in."

The first thing Me Susane noticed in the apartment was her orange scarf, hanging on the hallway coatrack.

She followed Sharon's husband into the tiny kitchen across from the rack, just to the right of the front door.

As warmly as possible, she turned down that frightened, thoughtful man's offer of coffee.

She didn't want to impose on him, didn't want to offend him or intimidate him or trouble him in any way at all.

The kitchen was shabby and clean, old and in a sense un-salvageable from the standpoint of contemporary hygiene, but scrubbed with such passion and relentlessness, Me Susane said to herself, that it seemed almost fresh, innocent.

"Sharon wasn't in my apartment earlier today, I was worried . . ."

"She must be at one of the other ladies'," said the husband, "she might have gotten the schedules mixed up, she does that."

"Yes, of course," said Me Susane, suddenly demolished.

"It's not easy," the husband dolefully went on. "The other ladies aren't easy to deal with like you are."

"Oh? What do you mean by that?"

Suddenly he fixed her with a dry, fevered gaze, and his amber face flushed red as he hesitated again, Me Susane realized, to speak freely.

That was why she also understood the vehemence in his voice when he next spoke: he was letting himself go, assuming, perhaps unreasonably, that Me Susane would prove an ally.

She'd sat down on a stiff little plastic chair.

She was still more stunned than irate—deceived, morosely hurt.

"The others, they call for her and Sharon has to go running," said the husband angrily. "Is that normal? Sharon can't be everywhere at once, she can't be here and there at the same time, isn't that right? She's worn out, she's worn out."

"These other women, how many are there?"

"Two ladies, with you that makes three, but," he clarified, "you always treat her right, not like the others."

"Why? What do they do?" asked Me Susane, her tone steady, almost offhand.

Her heart was bleeding.

She'd never heard a word about the other ladies, she'd never dreamt that rather than put in her hours at the apartment where Me Susane generously paid her to stay (there was so little to clean!) Sharon might covertly take work elsewhere.

Wasn't that small of her?

Wasn't it understandable, all the same?

And wasn't it only proper that Sharon should dupe Me Susane, who thought she had the right to keep her there in her apartment, thinking that boredom and wasted time were of no importance next to the good salary she paid her and the work she was doing to help Sharon's family stay legally in France?

But her heart was bleeding.

Now Sharon's husband was slumped in another of the old lawn chairs that surrounded the table, roughly rubbing the tabletop back and forth, as if to scour it, or to punish it for not being clean or beautiful enough.

Monsieur and Madame Susane had the same sort of table in their little backyard, Me Susane thought distractedly.

Oh, how she ached, how Sharon was hurting her!

"Those other ladies," the husband bristled, "they don't

count all Sharon's hours, and they don't talk to her nicely either, they're never happy, even though no one works harder than Sharon, isn't that so?"

"Yes," Me Susane murmured, "Sharon's work is always perfect."

"Right, that's just what I'm saying."

He'd raised his voice, as if Me Susane had contradicted him.

She didn't move, looked away.

Across the street, leaning on the railing of his decrepit window, a man was watching them with a cigarette between his lips.

His gaze struck Me Susane as disapproving.

Reflexively, she forced herself to comfort Sharon's husband.

She put her hand on his forearm, kneaded it gently.

She'd understood, or presumed from the few reserved words Sharon had spoken on the subject of her husband, that he'd "gone into a depression" (as Monsieur and Madame Susane were in the habit of saying) not long after their move to France.

For fear of being arrested and asked for papers he didn't have, he hid away at home, furtively going out only to pick up the children from school when Sharon couldn't make it.

He didn't know and never saw anyone but his wife and his children, which, Sharon had reflected with a disconsolate sigh, would be enough, anywhere in the world, to unsettle the mind of the sturdiest man.

"I'd go crazy too if I were in his shoes!" Sharon had exclaimed.

Me Susane asked her nothing more.

Direct questions upset Sharon, they left her silent, suspicious, and her eyelids with their long, thick lashes began to blink painfully.

Me Susane would have said to her: It's just as dangerous, Sharon, for you to go out and work as it is for your husband. And suppose you're arrested, suppose you're investigated, what can your husband do? He'll be sent back the same as you, what will protect him? So why does he leave it entirely to you to do the things that have to be done to live a normal life, why are you the only one who works, the only one who goes out shopping, the only one who risks a run-in with the police, in short the only one who actually makes an effort?

Sharon, thought Me Susane, would have answered in her shocked, virtuous voice: But he's sad, he's sick! He's sick with sadness, he can't help it.

"These other ladies, do you know their names?" she gently asked Sharon's husband.

She leaned forward, bringing her face closer to his.

He wiped his cheeks and lips on his sleeve in a childish gesture that she couldn't help being moved by.

"Do you know my name?" she asked.

"Yes, of course." He gave a little laugh at the obviousness of the question. "You're Madame Susane, and the others are Madame Pujol and Madame Principaux. How would I not know the names of the women exploiting Sharon? I don't mean you, Madame Susane. But the other two, they're exploiting her and Sharon doesn't know what to do to get herself out of it. For example, do you know what Madame Principaux did one day? She said Sharon hadn't vacuumed completely under the rug, she'd only turned back the corners, and that wasn't acceptable, so as punishment she didn't get her day's pay."

Mᵉ Susane clasped her trembling hands.

She sensed that her face had gone a dull gray, as always when she was particularly shocked.

"Principaux?" she murmured. "Where does she live, this Principaux woman? In Caudéran? In Le Bouscat?"

A beautiful villa in Le Bouscat had been the home of Gilles and Marlyne Principaux and their children.

"No, no," said Sharon's husband, faintly impatient, "she lives in the city, in the neighborhood by the cathedral. She's an old lady, her husband is dead, she lives there all alone, she's rich, and she finds ways to abuse Sharon. I can't stand seeing people take advantage of Sharon, she doesn't know how to defend herself, she always says yes and thank you."

So that's why Sharon is deceiving me, Mᵉ Susane thought feverishly, that's why she lets me think she's spent the afternoon in my place when in fact she went to the others', because she doesn't know how to get free of those other two "ladies."

Yes, that's it, she's trapped, she's trapped, poor Sharon, Mᵉ Susane told herself over and over in such an ecstasy of relief that her trembling grew still more violent.

"I have to go now," she said, cautiously standing up.

Sharon's husband gave her a wave without moving from his chair.

In the front hall, Mᵉ Susane slipped the orange scarf off the coatrack, stuffed it in her bag, and left as discreetly as if she'd done something wrong.

From there she went straight to the office, not stopping by her apartment.

She preferred not to have to find Sharon possibly absent, not to have to catch Sharon in the act again—because she knew, so what would that change?

And if Sharon were there, what difference would it make?

Since either way Sharon was sneaking out on her.

But it wasn't her fault, it was because of those Pujol and Principaux women who'd found in her the perfect slave!

Me Susane quivered with anger.

Was this Principaux woman Gilles's mother?

If so, she'd changed a great deal—that marvelous, winning, welcoming woman in her beautiful Caudéran house, who, in such a graciously everyday way, with such unfeigned pleasure, had offered the ironing woman's daughter an orange juice!

Were there, in Bordeaux, other families named Principaux than this one?

Me Susane hoped so, gloomily, fiercely.

In the office, eager to be done with it, she busied herself answering the little mail she'd gotten.

Me Susane, newly in business for herself, worked alone.

She'd taken the step of renting two beautiful rooms on the cathedral square, thinking a distinguished address and a well-appointed office would bring in an interesting clientele—but, my God, it was so hard!

When her clients paid her, it was only after a long delay, every time.

Me Susane liked to tell her friends, the ones who invited her for dinner and appreciated her talent at telling stories, her wry humor (which to her seemed so forced!), that she loved combat but hated conflict, and so found it very difficult to claim what she was owed.

What a chore it all was!

She printed out every article she could find on the Principaux case, the ones she'd already read back when Marlyne was arrested, which she still remembered so clearly she could almost recite them, and a few others from what she considered vaguely distasteful websites, which she read with some unease but which, as the sentences went by, seemed to have discerned an obscure truth: the husband's indulgence, his eagerness to try to "free his wife from her demons" after the killings (or murders) were carried out.

Because Gilles Principaux seemed not so much devastated by the death of his children as bent on absolving Marlyne in the eyes of the world.

And why not? thought Me Susane.

And what did it mean to be "devastated," what unambiguous conclusion was there to be drawn from Gilles Principaux's dry eyes, his strange smiles before the cameras, his obvious pleasure in holding forth on the horror of it all?

According to what unassailable criteria, both moral and psychological, could one conclude, simply because he smiled abundantly, that his children's death did not affect him as deeply as it should?

Those unsavory, vengeful sites had put their finger on one

true thing, thought Me Susane: Gilles Principaux had an unusual reaction to the event that was supposed to have shattered his existence.

He seemed strangely sunny, excited, pleased with himself, then turned tearful when he sensed he was expected to be bereft, broken, changed, and his tears or their simulation seemed ungenuine, because he wasn't good at acting what he didn't feel: bereft, broken, changed.

But those peculiarities should not lead to any judgment of Gilles Principaux's pain, thought Me Susane.

Who are you to dictate the form my sorrow has to take? How do you know how sad I feel, have you burrowed into my heart?

All the respectable newspaper articles that Me Susane recalled almost verbatim described the same scene: two police officers, a man and a woman, entering the home of Gilles and Marlyne Principaux after the latter had telephoned and urgently asked for someone to come, though her calm, cold voice, with no particular intonation to it, seemed to contradict the need for the officers to hurry.

They rang the doorbell, knocked, then, getting no answer, simply opened the unlocked door.

They found Marlyne sitting up very straight on the living room couch.

The house was tidy, almost excessively tidy, one of them would later say (expressing, thought Me Susane, more that officer's own relationship with housework than anything odd about Marlyne).

Marlyne greeted them in a steady voice, thanked them for coming.

Sitting stock-still, she very quietly told them to go to her room, at the end of the hallway.

She was gentle and calm, a bit pale (one of the two would later say, but how to know her usual tint?), and the only sign that she might be on edge was the way she pressed her hands between her clenched thighs.

One of the two would also say that her gaze was slightly wild.

Although her neighbors and friends would say of Marlyne that despite her sedate way of moving, of speaking, her eyes were always restless, darting about like the eyes of a bird watching for danger—like, one neighbor would say, the look in a titmouse's eyes when it flies from a branch to the nest where its hungry chicks are calling.

No sooner did that neighbor speak those words than she clapped her hand to her mouth, because titmice don't murder their young, do they?

The two officers, a middle-aged man, potbellied and solid, following a young, sporty woman, headed toward the Princi- pauxs' bedroom, down a hallway of closed doors.

The woman found the three children lying in their parents' bed.

Me Susane wasn't sure, after reading these serious articles, if the children were lying on the bed and entirely visible to the policewoman or if their mother had slipped them under the covers with only their heads sticking out.

None of the articles were clear on that point.

Some said "in the bed," some said "on the bed," as if that were a detail of no importance.

The officer would say she saw immediately the children were dead.

Nonetheless, of course, she raced to the bed, tried to revive them as her colleague looked on, her colleague who said he was "in a state of deep shock, having three grandchildren of similar ages, and coincidentally, like the Principauxs, two boys and a girl still a baby."

The oldest one, Jason, was holding in his arms—or rather (Me Susane mentally corrected) had his arms around—his little sister, Julia, aged six months.

He was six years old; his brother, John, four.

The three children were naked, their skin dry, their hair damp and neatly combed.

The policewoman would say she could tell at one glance that they'd been in good health; their bodies were beautiful and well-formed, at once filled-out and delicate—children who'd been thoughtfully fed, whose flesh showed no sign of mistreatment.

The staged tenderness with which the oldest was holding the baby, protecting her, left the policewoman speechless, since, she grasped at once, death had not taken these children in that bed or in that position, and Marlyne Principaux would later say, with the false modesty of a mother who knows she's a paragon, that she had indeed taken the time and the trouble to arrange the children's bodies that way: Jason adored and spoiled the baby Julia, it was only right and true to display them in each other's arms.

As for John, she'd laid him on his side, with his pretty face turned toward the older brother he loved to the point of veneration.

"I tried not to get anything wrong," Marlyne would murmur with a humble smile, "not to betray them in their feelings, I knew them so well, no one knew them better than I did."

Stunned, the two police officers called for backup.

Marlyne Principaux, serene if slightly unsteady in her gait (as if she'd been drinking, but she hadn't), took them to the still-full bathtub, explained as willingly as an obedient schoolchild how she'd drowned first the baby Julia and then John, and finally Jason, who struggled so forcefully that she'd had to get into the bathtub herself, hold his legs down with her knees, wrestle with him in a burst of violence that she'd hated.

"I didn't foresee that, I so wanted not to hurt him, not to hurt anyone, especially my beloved child!" Marlyne would say, horrified at the memory.

It would seem obvious to everyone who heard her that she'd done her best not to inflict any unnecessary pain (knowing that they would after all be dying) on those three children she claimed to love more than anything.

She would say she'd done some research on the internet: the surest way to put an end to them ("to send them to heaven," she said) without harming their bodies was to drown them.

She knew perfectly well that the two boys must have felt overwhelming terror and despair, must have felt deep horror and incomprehension, as she pressed their faces down into the water with both hands to keep them at the bottom of the tub.

She closed her eyes at that point, she would say.

Me Susane didn't believe it.

She reread the articles and found herself seized by an anger that hadn't visited her at the time of the events.

She didn't believe that Marlyne Principaux kept her eyes closed all through those long minutes when she was methodically, doggedly drowning the children.

With Jason and John, it wasn't easy.

They were sturdy, energetic boys, why would they consent to their own murder?

Marlyne could only have done the job with exertion and brutality, with grunting and splashing, with pleas and resistance, she couldn't have kept her eyes closed (like a martyred saint) all through the act.

What was the nature of that act?

Only hate, Me Susane told herself, can make such an atrocity tolerable to its perpetrator.

Because, it had to be said, Marlyne had tortured her three children, hadn't she?

Me Susane was badly shaken.

In the opinion of all her close acquaintances, even those who would curse her, who would want nothing more to do with her (her mother, her sisters), Marlyne doted on her sons, particularly, perhaps (but what meaning to ascribe to that possible preference?), the older one, Jason, of whom she seemed (perhaps) excessively proud.

Nonetheless, those very acquaintances would hurry to add that she also displayed a zealous love for John and Julia, always worrying over their health, she was still nursing the baby at the time of the killings (or murders) and had in fact breastfed her only a few minutes before.

What did all that mean? Me Susane wondered.

Marlyne Principaux had drowned her children in the late afternoon, not long after she'd picked the boys up from school, sat them all down for their afternoon snack in the kitchen as she did every day, and, as almost every day in the life of that admirable mother, served them each a slice of orange-flavored pound cake baked just for them.

She would say that she never allowed herself to feed her children any food she hadn't made herself, which is why Jason and John didn't eat in the school lunchroom.

Every day at twenty minutes to noon, Marlyne laid Julia into the pram and walked to the school, coming home with the boys and then accompanying them back before the 1:30 bell, still with Julia, whom she'd taken care to nurse just beforehand (to keep her quiet during the walk, she would explain).

Every day she made them a rigorously balanced lunch, not only calculating the proper number of calories for children of four and six but also gauging the proteins, carbohydrates, and lipids to be sure she was providing all the nourishment they needed.

She measured her own meals in the same way, to promote Julia's growth, since she intended to nurse her daughter for a full two years, as she had her sons.

To her great despair (though she never revealed it to anyone, not even her husband, whom she told everything), Marlyne Principaux regularly gained weight in spite of her excellent diet.

And at the time of the killings (or murders) she found herself facing this dilemma: whether to actively try to slim down and thus risk passing on to Julia a milk less perfectly adapted to the little girl's harmonious development or keep to the regimen most suited to a thriving baby but detrimental, she thought, to her own figure.

She was so ashamed to be fretting over such a trivial matter!

Particularly because neither her husband nor her friends seemed to notice she was putting on weight.

But Marlyne did.

She saw it when she was dressing, when she soaped her body in the shower, and so she resolved never again to put on her usual clothes.

At the Emmaus secondhand shop, she bought a few men's T-shirts and pullovers, along with two enormous pairs of elastic-waist trousers, thanks to which she could dull her awareness of her body's bulges and perpetually spreading contours.

Was she happy in those clothes?

Not exactly, but at least she could forget herself, which is what she wanted, so that she could escape the terror of knowing she was expanding and couldn't do anything about it.

Because it would be unthinkable to stop nursing Julia.

Oh my God!

Marlyne would almost have laughed at the idea, perhaps.

Endanger the baby's health for such an insignificant reason!

Who could think of such a thing?

She might just as well take to drink, or to drugs, she might just as well beat and neglect her children!

Once you start worrying not about them but about yourself, where does it end?

Reading the papers, Me Susane had seen only the summary of the events, the police's discovery of the crime, the account of Marlyne's first words.

All the rest she was inventing, presuming, but, she would discover later, with what astonishing clairvoyance!

In spite of her deep dislike, even her repulsion for Marlyne Principaux!

After they'd tried and failed to revive the children, the two officers joined Marlyne in the living room, where she was still sitting in the same position, straight and meek, her hands folded, her smile polite, fixed, regretful.

She was wearing a voluminous T-shirt with the insignia of the Sorbonne, and dull gray sweatpants that pooled over the tops of her tennis shoes.

The policewoman would notice two damp spots on the cotton of her shirt, just over her breasts, and, spotting her glance, Marlyne would say apologetically that her milk was flowing.

It was November, the day was gray and mild, the house was well-heated, perhaps too well.

The officers soon found themselves sweating, but (Me Susane would wonder) was it the temperature or was it their emotion, who could say with any certainty?

Suddenly Gilles Principaux came in, hurried, anxious.

"Everything OK, my love?" he called out toward Marlyne (a character straight out of a sitcom, Me Susane would think, innocently showing up at the scene of a crime and speaking words that ring false even though they're simply the way he talks).

Marlyne gave him a closed-mouth smile.

She looked down and vaguely waved at him, as if to reassure him.

It would be learned that she'd called her husband an hour before she called the police, asking him to please come home, because she had a problem.

Gilles Principaux should have gotten there before the two officers, but, even though there were no classes at that time, he had various administrative questions to deal with, which delayed his start back to Le Bouscat, a bit put out (he would admit) at having to jump into his car and come home before the usual time.

It was when he saw the police parked in front of the house that he became afraid.

"Everything OK, my love?" he called out, not yet suspecting anything (as he would say, because how could any husband imagine such an abomination, such a betrayal of the harmony and openness that, they would both affirm, always reigned in their relationship?).

And Marlyne smiled at him, although, he observed, with a certain hesitation, with some effort.

Nonetheless, she'd made that assuaging little gesture he knew well: she slapped the air with a limp, confident, slightly ironic hand, which meant "nothing serious, my love, everything's under control."

That was a private code between them: whenever Gilles

walked in on a turbulent scene, the few times when her paren-
tal attentions had created disorder in the house, or when the
boys, inexplicably agitated, wanted to fight and seemed suddenly to loathe each other (how that always hurt Marlyne!),
she gave Gilles that little sign.

And then, miraculously, everything was set to rights again.

Jason and John stopped lashing out at each other for no reason, Julia accepted the breast that she'd not long before hurt-
fully pushed away, the living room was suddenly straightened
and tidy without Marlyne or Gilles (manifestly) seeing to it.

Was that a supernatural effect of their thought, of their will?

Marlyne was not far from thinking so.

The more down-to-earth Gilles would say that no one had
ever found the house in disarray.

Cleanliness was an obsession for Marlyne, he'd gotten used
to it.

She was quick to see a room full of life as a horrifying chaos,
and the boys' fights demoralized her as if they bore witness to
her failure as a parent.

She was absolutely obsessive, Gilles would say, quite openly,
intending no criticism.

Marlyne would say that Gilles couldn't stand seeing things
"in a mess," and that it was for him, for his serenity, and to fore-
stall any irritation on his part, any simmering reproach, that
she took anxious pains to be sure that the house but also life in
general were perfectly orderly.

In her toneless voice, she would express a resentment of
him, sometimes even a sort of detached, disdainful hatred, a
strange hatred without passion.

Not him.

He would defend her against all reason, without detachment, with passion.

And so, in Me Susane's imagination, in her speculations, in her musings, portraits began to take shape of a Gilles Principaux convinced of his own easygoing attitude toward the organization of the family's day-to-day life and a Marlyne equally sure that she had to provide her husband the tranquility he tacitly demanded.

Marlyne would later say:

"Every day I thought of him coming home and I was afraid. I didn't want him to be annoyed or irritated because things weren't just as they should be. He was nice, yes, he never spoke a cruel word. But I could feel his disappointment, his displeasure when I hadn't done well, couples can feel these things about each other, you don't say anything but you feel everything, you understand everything."

It would later come out that, after her children were born and she stopped working (at Gilles's urging, she would assert), Marlyne had closed herself up in the idea that since she was no longer engaged in her profession as a middle school French teacher she had to show her husband, her mother (who was angry to see her daughter stop working, stop striving for excellence and independence), and her sisters that motherhood was work just as admirable, just as difficult, just as worthy of respect as teaching.

She wanted to be a top-class mother, like an athlete, Me Susane would tell herself.

Marlyne and her two sisters had been raised by their mother

alone, and everything that had to do with their father was nebulous—had he walked out, had he been thrown out, the mother never offered her thoughts on that question.

Marlyne's mother merely claimed, rightly, that she'd successfully brought up her daughters in spite of the difficulties inherent in her situation as a single woman with a modest income.

She worked in the vineyards as a laborer, and if Marlyne, the object of her greatest pride before the marriage to Principaux, had become a teacher, her two sisters hadn't disappointed their mother's expectations either, the youngest working as a cellar master, the middle child as manager of a clothes shop.

Yes, Me Susane would think admiringly, that simple, courageous woman had given her daughters a higher place on the social ladder, overseeing their schooling as best she could, meeting with the teachers (too often, some would say—or was Me Susane inventing that detail? She didn't know anymore), allowing them to spend time only with people worthy of her own ambitions and sacrifices, and perhaps excessively severe at times but how can that be helped when you live in a little apartment in the outskirts of Langon and you know that your teenaged daughters dream of being allowed to hang around the massive shopping center after class, since the high school is right next door to the big-box zone, and well-informed acquaintances have told you that it was there, in the still-vacant lots between the Intermarché and the Lidl, that young people drank, smoked, shot up, lived that brief period of their existence in such a way that their life would remain forever smaller, shadowed and spoiled, and people would say of them: What a shame!

Marlyne's mother had fought to make sure that no one could

ever say of her three intelligent, talented daughters: What a shame!

Was she a hard mother, excessively inflexible?

One article insinuated just that.

Marlyne's mother and two sisters would refuse to see her after the killings (or murders).

But their visits had already grown rare after Marlyne's children were born, as if Marlyne had failed beyond repair by choosing that kind of life, and indeed the sisters had never had children, although Me Susane wasn't sure if that was their choice.

In any case, neither the mother nor the sisters had seemed profoundly and painfully stricken by the loss of Jason, John, and Julia, who, in the end, they knew only distantly.

But Marlyne's grotesque fall into mediocrity had mortified them for all time.

Me Susane even had the impression that all three of them, mother and sisters, could endure the horror of Marlyne's act, that they could imagine the scene without feeling invaded by that horror.

What they could not forgive Marlyne, thought Me Susane, was that she'd fled so far from them in spirit by marrying Principaux, abandoning her career to raise Principaux's children, in short that she'd complied with all the spoken or unspoken injunctions of that Principaux man who'd been clever enough, on that score at least (the sisters and mother told themselves, according to Me Susane), to marry a social inferior.

"She never dared contradict him," one of the sisters would say.

And the other:

"He had her cowed, he came from the bourgeoisie, behind that fake cool of his he was actually quite the authoritarian."

And the mother:

"He found all sorts of ways to convince her she wasn't worth much, he completely crushed her self-confidence. I didn't recognize her when I went to see her so I stayed away, it was too much for me to bear. She used to love her work, teaching French in middle school, and now here she was blathering at me that there was no finer mission than to be a mama, that she wanted to do everything she could to protect her children from this world's dangers, blah blah blah, that you couldn't live up to that glorious mission unless you were a mama full-time, blah blah blah. I was furious at her, I decided to keep my distance, all that work for nothing, I kept telling myself, what a waste. And I knew Principaux was behind that change in her, I knew the Marlyne I'd brought up to be free, who put that freedom to good use until she was twenty-six, when Principaux got his hooks into her, I knew she would never have chosen that kind of life on her own, I knew it but there was no way I could get through to Marlyne, because Principaux had her in his spell, she was always mindlessly singing his praises, Gilles was wonderful, blah blah blah, Gilles was so smart, blah blah blah, Gilles always did such sweet little things for her, blah blah blah. She forced herself to say all that, she was sad and lost, she didn't want to face it, she had her pride. So I kept away from her, and her sisters did the same. There's nothing you can do in cases like that. She would have ended up hating us, she would have ended up tossing us out. Principaux couldn't stand us. He must have whispered all kinds of vicious things about us in her ear. I'm unhappy, and I'm terribly sorry for Marlyne, who'll never be free again, who'll never again teach French in middle school as she so loved to do. Of course, it's terrible about those poor kids who never did a thing to anyone. I'm not yet ready to go visit Marlyne, I'm still too mad at her. Those poor kids, yes, of course. But I'm mad at Marlyne for wanting to get away from us, her mother and sisters, to embrace the Principaux spirit, to join that glorious Principaux family, whose son, Gilles, subjugated her plain and simple. Yes, she let him, she went along with it, but she didn't know what she was doing. Should I have stayed by her side? It wasn't possible, like I said, she would have ended up finding some pretext to keep us estranged for the rest of our lives."

Then Gilles Principaux came in, impatient, irritable, agitated.

He wasn't happy about having to come home early from the Université de Bordeaux, where he taught geography, but all at once an alarm crept into his annoyance (the police car parked in front of his building), and he raced toward Marlyne, fearing, he would say quite convincingly, that his wife was injured or ill.

Not for one moment, he would say, was he afraid for the children.

Because he loved his wife more than anyone on earth, yes, even more than the children, for whom he did of course feel great affection.

But it was Marlyne who caused him his most anguished anxieties and most powerful surges of love.

To his mind the children would always get by, with their

voracious vitality, like little animals, all of them graced with a good health, a physical well-being, a bodily perfection that hadn't given him the habit of trembling for them.

No, he'd never felt any morbid forebodings about them.

Perhaps he sometimes felt almost submerged by their greedy appetite for existence, their imperious will to be there, in his life, and by the fact that their dense, domineering little bodies cared nothing about his, its weaknesses and fatigues, wanting only to grow as comfortably as possible, in the shelter of their father's body, of course, their father from whom they innocently, savagely drew the substance necessary for their relentless life.

Gilles Principaux was exhausted by his young children.

Nonetheless, he wanted more, he wanted many children, perhaps five or six in all.

But he never feared for them.

He'd never had one of those cruel dreams where you see your children in danger.

On the other hand, he dreaded the frequent nightmare in which Marlyne lay dying far from him and he knew it but couldn't go to her and Marlyne died without having one last time been assured of his love.

That was how Gilles Principaux talked, Me Susane gathered, with strings of beautiful, sincere sentences, saying strange and sometimes uncomfortable things, which at least seemed perfectly candid, whereas Principaux's smiling, exaggeratedly guileless face gave an impression of duplicity that was just as uncomfortable.

"Why did you want to add to your family," he would be

asked, "when you already had difficulty looking after three children? When, by your own account, you already found it quite hard to mete out your affection? To offer it equally to everyone in that little world?"

"I wanted more because I sensed very strongly it was Marlyne's wish," Principaux would answer.

Asked the same question, Marlyne would recognize that she'd longed for their first child, Jason, but would have preferred he remain the only one.

She never dared admit that to Gilles, nor explicitly to herself, because the unspoken pact that founded their union, the purpose of those two very different people living together, was bound up with the ambition of procreating in great numbers and great joy, untouched by anything like religion, on the contrary, they were atheists, came from families with no faith and believed they had every right to give France beautiful children in a spirit of wholly secular delight (as they liked to say, with a smile).

Then Gilles Principaux came in, and the policewoman would say that terror could be read on his face.

For a moment he was reassured by Marlyne's presence: sitting on the couch, still herself, not sick or wounded or despairing, a little stiff and distant perhaps, but Gilles Principaux never studied Marlyne so closely when he came home from campus that he could distinguish one evening from the evening before, one mood from the evening before's.

This was how Marlyne usually was, reserved, not very talkative.

People said she was dreary and anxious at the same time, the very few people who met her now and then but could in no way claim to be that solitary woman's friends: pupils' parents, high school classmates she sometimes ran into in the street.

Marlyne and Gilles would observe aloud, both of them in open and honest agreement, and as if they'd never noticed it before, that Marlyne had no friends.

There were sort-of friends, Gilles's friends, whom he asked over for dinner or coffee, though not often, because Gilles, when he wasn't working, liked "peace and quiet."

Those friends of Gilles's, the only ones Marlyne would mention as being also vaguely her friends, could be counted on one hand.

Marlyne would have difficulty remembering their names.

She would even mix up their genders, misremembering Gilles's colleague Frédérique as a man, having no memory of the two or three times Frédérique called on them, and lying like a child when her name was spoken:

"Yes, Frédéric, I remember he was nice, I liked him."

And those people (friends?) whom Gilles Principaux seemed to somewhat reluctantly invite over would say of Marlyne that they had to confess they'd scarcely paid her any mind.

She was so diffident!

Polite and drab, very formally welcoming, with her tortured, shifting gaze that made you want to look away.

She was awkward to be around, no one quite knew what to say to her, and the questions they asked out of politeness offered no opening for further conversation: she answered carefully, never returning the question, indifferent or ill at ease.

Her mother and sisters would say she was a lively, talkative young woman before she met Principaux.

Two people who believed they knew her well in her days as a literature student in Bordeaux would concur: Marlyne was spirited, voluble but not to excess, and with her bright clothes, her tidy makeup, her awareness of the splendor of her dark blond hair, she was not a diffident girl, on the contrary: she loved to charm, to be admired, she laughed often, she was open, loyal, pretty, "happy with who she was."

Those two witnesses (male, female, Me Susane couldn't tell which) would admit that it had taken them some time to realize the Marlyne from their student days was the Marlyne in that horrible news story.

Marlyne's former colleagues would say the same.

She'd spent only eighteen months at that middle school in Pauillac, but they'd had many opportunities to chat with her and to hear what the students said of her, more than enough to establish that she was a good-hearted person and a fabulous teacher, so they too saw no connection between their former colleague and the monstrous heroine of that news story, until certain details left them no choice.

Marlyne Principaux quit the school in Pauillac when she became pregnant for the first time.

She never went back.

In a lighthearted email, with a comical-ironic enthusiasm that might have seemed forced to those who knew her (but did anyone know her? wondered Me Susane, her jaw clenched, her heart pounding), Marlyne had told three or four teachers of Jason's birth, of her wish to devote herself entirely to "that wonderful little boy's first steps in life," and then she'd stopped writing.

They wanted to send a gift, to visit her, to celebrate the event somehow.

She wouldn't cooperate.

She evaded, stalled, finally stopped answering.

They concluded, with some disappointment, that she wanted "peace and quiet."

With some disappointment, they forgot about her.

They were all (not that there were many of them) offended by her disengagement.

"She clearly didn't want anything more to do with us," an English teacher would say. "We couldn't understand why, because we had an excellent relationship with Marlyne."

They would conclude, later, that Gilles Principaux was responsible for her distance.

Wasn't that unfair?

Because Principaux's version of the facts would be entirely different.

He said he urged Marlyne to invite her colleagues over, to introduce the baby, he would even say he was bewildered and almost humiliated, as the baby's father, that his wife stubbornly refused (although without saying so, inert and closed, silent but immoveable) to proudly show what was after all the glorious fruit of their equally glorious union.

On Marlyne's side, only her mother and sisters would come and see Jason, not very often once they realized Marlyne wasn't planning to go back to work, when they all three began to feel the same anger at her, an anger that wouldn't let them come back and visit her "as if everything were fine."

Marlyne would confirm Principaux's statement: he had indeed pushed her to ask her colleagues over, he'd raised the possibility of a dinner or an aperitif hour when he might finally meet those four or five teachers from the school in Pauillac whom Marlyne had worked with and liked, Marlyne would confirm that, Principaux had brought it up several times.

She said nothing, did nothing, invited no one, and Principaux gave up, forgot.

"I was too tired, too worn out to arrange any gatherings, I would have had to do all the work, Gilles was too busy," Marlyne would say.

And then:

"I thought that deep down he'd rather it not happen, I sensed that he felt nothing but contempt for my colleagues, that the very idea of having a drink with them bored him unbearably, he would have put up a good front and no one would have seen anything (that disdain, that boredom), but I thought it would be simpler not to force us all to endure that little charade of camouflaged hypocrisy and meanness (on Gilles's part), it's easier to do nothing than labor to put together something that could easily turn out to be uncomfortable or disappointing or annoying, that's why I didn't do anything, didn't say anything, didn't answer, oh, it's my fault, because Gilles was encouraging me to organize something he couldn't stand the thought of, he was biting the bullet, he thought he was being nice to me. But I knew him so well, he had no idea how well! I never would have put my colleagues from Pauillac through the ordeal of Gilles's silent, sarcastic judgment, oh, it's my fault, Gilles has nothing to do with it, he is how he is, that's all, and I loved him as he was, what fault can I find with him? Apart from making me fear him and loathe him, but am I not responsible for my mistake, the mistake of having loved him, followed him, of having abandoned my judgment for his, of having thought that any little idea, opinion, or preference I had might trigger 'the nullity clause' [she was laughing when she said that, surely?] if Gilles didn't approve of it?

"It's my fault," Marlyne would say, "because most of the time Gilles was perfectly nice to me, he tried to help me with the children even if he was tired, or at least he asked if I wanted his help, and I generally said no, but I liked being asked and he knew it and he wasn't ungenerous with offers like that.

"Deep down," Marlyne would say, "I have no complaints about Gilles. I started to find myself tensing up when I heard him come home in the evening, I came to dread his honeyed nitpicking and his very firm positions on the raising of our children and our way of life, the morality he insisted we embrace, but I don't hold him responsible. I didn't talk much. I didn't express myself clearly. How could he ever have guessed that I couldn't stand the children anymore, that I prayed Gilles might die with them in an accident so I could find myself free and sad, free and heartsick and finally delivered of his all-knowing eye, of Gilles's gaze probing me and faulting me even with his lips pulled back in an eternal smile?

"I'm not blaming Gilles Principaux," Marlyne would conclude. "I'd like never to see him again, I feel no compassion or fondness for him, but I'm not blaming him. He never did anything you could call ignoble. He sincerely aspired to be an excellent person, a good father, a good husband, there's nothing wicked about Gilles Principaux, and if I came to abhor him, to dream of his death (or his erasure, his sudden and permanent absence from my life), I blame only my weakness, not his.

"I beseech you," Marlyne would say (hands joined, eyelids trembling), "don't be tempted to implicate Gilles Principaux in my guilt, don't try to partially absolve me by condemning that poor man who on top of the unthinkable blow he has suffered would also have to explain (which inevitably he wouldn't do convincingly) why he doesn't believe he played some dark role in the horror that's come to him."

No, neither Gilles nor Marlyne would accuse the other, which, given the circumstances, might seem suspicious, particularly on Gilles's part.

Why did he seem to feel no anger at his villainous wife?

Why try to defend her over the interests, morally speaking, of their murdered (or dead) children, three innocents?

He seemed almost ready to accuse the children in his wife's defense, evoking, though vaguely, elliptically, Jason's difficult personality, John's inexplicable rages, even (though only once) the baby Julia's "egocentrism."

No more than Marlyne with him, Gilles Principaux found no fault with her.

Only for killing (or murdering) their children could he condemn his wife.

In every other way he loved and admired her, he would say.

He'd never had any serious problems with Marlyne.

And, since this question couldn't be eluded or prevented, they would both answer as one: their sex life was fantastic (for her), terrific (for him).

They'd always been perfectly matched in that regard, at once playful and wholesome and always, they would say, "mindful of the other's desires."

Gilles had never forced Marlyne and Marlyne had never obligated Gilles to do anything at all, although in her words she hated him at the end, wanted to see him dead along with the children through no fault of her own, wanted to be free and innocent—whereas the choice she'd made left her free and monstrously guilty.

Principaux would be judged excessively loyal to Marlyne, so much so that he would be accused of duplicity, of supporting his wife for his own ends.

Me Susane thought no such thing.

Principaux's pain simply took an unusual form, she concluded.

Did her own sorrows not take indiscernible forms, forms that could deceive those who thought they knew her best?

Principaux's attitude would shock the two police officers, who were marked for life by the sight of the dead children.

Because he refused to be protected from that sight, he insisted (he would almost have fought for it, physically) on seeing the children lying in the bedroom.

Then he nearly fainted, although that's not certain.

The policewoman would say she saw him stagger, saw him cling to the doorjamb.

According to her colleague he was perfectly steady on his feet, and Principaux himself wouldn't remember anything, suggesting that his faintness was the very cause of that amnesia.

But only the female officer would claim Principaux had tottered when he first saw the dead children, in or on his own paternal bed, the very place where, in the course of a healthy, rapturous erotic life, he had begotten those three perfect little bodies.

Her colleague would contradict her on that point, and although his account was neutral it would be seen as further evidence of Principaux's strange coldness, such that, Me Susane noted, the woman who'd committed the crime, the woman who had (as some said) "performed" the homicidal or murderous act would seem less blameworthy than the father with his surprising reactions.

As a subject of fascination, the question of why that man behaved as he did outweighed, in certain articles, the killer's motives.

After Principaux, reeling or not, normally devastated or not quite devastated enough (his face haggard, the policewoman would say, rather calm, her colleague would say, could a face not, Me Susane wondered, be at once calm and haggard?), left the bedroom where his children were laid out (he'd come no farther than the doorway, hadn't approached the bed), he went back to Marlyne, sank onto the sofa beside her.

That with once glance he'd clearly grasped the situation troubled the police officers still more.

He asked no questions, didn't want to know how it happened, didn't play the part, Me Susane understood, of the unsuspecting victim.

Could he, even then, still have been thinking it was a "domestic accident"?

The two police officers would say that hypothesis never entered their minds, not for a moment did they think this sensible, sober, lucid man might believe his three children had died together by accident in the same tubful of water.

It was simply that Principaux didn't seem "emotional" enough.

Nonetheless, he asked the policewoman (her colleague wouldn't remember this clearly, but Marlyne would confirm it, albeit in her hesitant, hazy way) if, had he come home sooner, if he'd climbed into his car the moment Marlyne asked him to come, he might have gotten there before Marlyne acted.

Could I have saved them, he must have asked, if I were here earlier?

Of course the policewoman couldn't say.

She didn't answer either way.

She patted him on the shoulder, she pitied that man but there was nothing she could do for him.

Me Susane spent her afternoon reading anything she could find on the Principaux case and taking fevered notes, imagining what she wasn't told, what for the moment no one could know.

· · ·

Night had long since fallen by the time she got home.

And although she'd stayed late at the office, although she'd taken her time walking home in the cold for no other reason than to avoid meeting up with Sharon, Sharon was still there when she came in, busy in the kitchen, her cheeks and brow oddly flushed.

A great weariness fell over Me Susane.

She didn't have it in her this evening to chat with Sharon.

"Sharon, it's very late, you have to go now," she said softly, looking away from the young woman's red face.

"Yes, the dinner's done, I'm just on my way out," Sharon answered.

Me Susane took the orange scarf from her bag, hung it on the coatrack.

Not looking at Me Susane, who was in any case feeling so exhausted that she found herself freezing up in a very welcome apathy, Sharon took down the orange scarf, wrapped it around her neck in a resolute, almost violent gesture, then left the apartment, after no doubt mumbling:

"See you tomorrow."

In the kitchen, Me Susane discovered something straight out of a fairy tale—or something to "give you a good case of the creeps," she would say to her friends, rolling her eyes to make it seem funny, even though at the time she'd felt not fright but pure, grateful euphoria.

She found it easier, with her friends, to poke fun at Sharon, because Sharon had the power to hurt her over nothing at all.

But when she walked into the kitchen she realized at once that Sharon had diligently endeavored to make her happy that evening, to seek her forgiveness for something she thought it best not to speak of, or something she was too ashamed to talk about not to find it easier to act, even if that meant baring her heart there in the kitchen.

On every flat surface, the drainboard, the shelves, the top of the refrigerator, even on the chair and the stool, which she'd taken the trouble of draping in a floral cloth, Sharon had set a bowl, a plate, or a miniature stewpot containing, Me Susane would discover, a dish of tremendous refinement.

Never had Sharon, who had always made her delicious dinners, cooked so lavishly for Me Susane.

There was only one helping of each dish, and each was different from its neighbor, which meant that Sharon had prepared, separately and in minuscule quantities, a dozen little feasts.

Me Susane didn't recognize most of the vessels, she was for instance quite sure she'd never owned anything like the tiny cast-iron brightly colored stewpots in which Sharon had served the hot dishes—adorable, silly, ostentatiously cute stewpots whose concept Me Susane condemned and which she knew cost a great deal of money.

Could Sharon conceivably have bought those four microscopic pots, those Japanese-motif bowls, those delicate, slightly concave plates that modestly but earnestly, feelingly (they were endowed with a soul!) offered themselves up to Me Susane's admiration?

The plates beckoned her amiably, congenially urged her to come closer.

They were made of fine porcelain, and their rims could not have been thinner, their opalescence subtler.

Never would have Me Susane have bought such beautiful dishware for herself.

She wouldn't have dared, it would have been unchaste, and in any case the idea would never have occurred to her, so she wouldn't have been denying herself in any way.

And now here were these azure bowls, these iridescent plates exposing their spirit to her.

We live when you look at us and touch us, so gaze on us, appreciate us as we deserve to be appreciated! Sharon's bowls were saying to Me Susane.

Awaken us, rouse us from the torpor we're cast into by insensitive stares! the bowls went on, crying out in silence.

And Me Susane delicately lifted every lid, to see and to smell what was beneath it: in the little sea-green stewpot two rabbit kidneys with garlic, onions, and a sprinkling of fresh coriander, in the little sky-blue stewpot a chicken thigh simmered in a creamy green (sorrel?) sauce, and in the little pale yellow stewpot asparagus risotto.

And on the plates, in the bowls, elegantly dished out by Sharon: (1) a salad of potatoes, arugula, and red onion, (2) a salad of sun-dried tomato and einkorn, (3) jellied chicken with carrots, leeks, and preserved lemon, (4) cold beef tenderloin with pepper and coarse salt and slices of cornichon, (5) cold fennel à la grecque, (6) cold mushrooms à la grecque (fresh button mushrooms, which, in à la grecque form, Me Susane had encountered only canned, a dubious gelatin-thickened concoction that her parents bought at the supermarket), (7) seared prawns, almost scorched, sprinkled with Szechwan pepper, (8) buckwheat Crozet pasta with Beaufort cheese shavings, (9) barely cooked tuna with toasted sesame seeds.

Although she would have preferred a quick dinner so she could get back to her reflections on Marlyne Principaux's case, Me Susane thought it her duty to savor every one of Sharon's dishes.

It was more than she could manage.

But she forced herself, she ate to the point of revulsion.

The mere thought of offending Sharon horrified her.

Even worse would be to cheat, to think of deceiving Sharon, throwing out what she didn't eat, sealing it away in a garbage bag that she would stuff into her briefcase.

No, food like that couldn't be wasted—such work, such a gift offered to Me Susane, and such expense!

No one who expresses apologies or regrets in that way can be answered with any valid reason for not accepting them completely, along with the effort, along with the small sacrifice that consent implies.

Me Susane carefully washed all the plates, the bowls, the pots, dried them, set them out on the table.

She'd eaten so much that it left her almost dizzy, as if she'd drunk to excess.

Then, with difficulty, she fell asleep, waking three times in the night, feeling heavy, crammed full, weakened, but as soon as she half consciously recalled the origin of that indisposition, a surge of gratitude and relief brought her closer to Sharon, and inwardly she gave her thanks.

Who, in Me Susane's adult existence, had ever bothered to honor her? Even if it brought with it indigestion and a difficult night?

These were dark days of ice and mist over Bordeaux.

Me Susane tried to recall as precisely as she could her afternoon at the Principauxs' (if that was their name) when she was ten years old and Gilles (if that was him) fourteen (possibly fifteen?).

In reality, she remembered that wondrous day so clearly that she sometimes doubted herself, doubted her memory.

Could it all really have happened that harmoniously?

And what about Monsieur Susane's intuition that she and her mother had both been duped and abused in that beautiful Caudéran house, could she put that down to jealousy or fear and some brute need to defend his sober ways against the lascivious dissolutions of the bourgeoisie?

Monsieur Susane was an upright man, a loyal husband and a steadfast father, and, deeply, a trusting man.

Why, then, did he sense something depraved in that episode, and how much credit should be given his perception of things?

She had memories, he had only impressions.

Why did she feel she had to defend her memories against Monsieur Susane's impressions?

Her recollections, as if muddied by her father's skepticism, now seemed less clear to her, less certain.

But Me Susane would not give in.

Only two people knew what had happened in that bedroom, the boy and herself.

Ill-equipped with his prejudices, with his skewed intuitions, Monsieur Susane had no right to influence her.

Or maybe he did, since she was his daughter and he loved her?

Me Susane slipped on the icy pavement more often than she should, she was walking too fast, distracted, preoccupied.

A little vein had lately taken to bulging on her forehead, flickering.

She could feel it living and beating like an ambassador for her heart, which kept mum—but the little messenger vein told the truth of that heart!

One evening in the long, cold, gloomy week that Me Susane spent waiting for Marlyne Principaux's official request for her services, she had dinner with Rudy, at his invitation, in a restaurant on the Rue Saint-Rémi where they both liked to call themselves regulars though they rarely ate there, since one never went without the other, and no employee ever seemed to recognize them, just as not one face ever seemed familiar to Rudy or Me Susane, which they explained by a furious rate of turnover among the staff, nevertheless conceding that even if it were the same waitress greeting them every time they likely wouldn't have realized it, so marked were their meetings at the Brasserie Bordelaise by a delicious but taxing intensity.

Me Susane had met Rudy at the legal firm that first hired her. Like her, he was just out of law school, anxious but openhearted, eager to prove himself and prepared for any sacrifice, qualities that Me Susane recognized as her own.

Every one of the young lawyers recruited by that highly respected firm on the Place de Tourny possessed those same virtues, with varying degrees of scintillation.

What had bound Me Susane and Rudy (as she understood, but not he) was that their respective backgrounds hadn't prepared them for such a career, such success, nor for working beside young people of the sort the firm had hired at the same time as them: the offspring of well-to-do families from the city center or wine-country estates.

Rudy's parents had worked in the vineyards of the Médoc.

They were Spanish, they'd settled in Margaux fifty-some years before.

Rudy's brothers and sisters had gone to work in the vineyards straight out of middle school.

But Rudy kept at it, went to high school, got his *baccalauréat* if only just, studied law, made it through all the tests.

Not a brilliant student but a slogger, undiscourageable, dogged, he always felt he'd just barely squeaked by, had been passed almost by mistake.

And indeed, his parents, more relieved than happy to hear of a new success, or, to their minds, of a failure deferred, always said to him:

"What a stroke of luck, my God, what a stroke of luck!"

Whereupon they began to dread the coming defeat, which would prove all the more total in that Rudy was denying his destiny as a farmworker's son and had set his sights, even if he trembled as he did so, on a station higher than his own.

And how he did tremble!

That he'd reached his goal, encouraged or hobbled by such meager confidence in his abilities, that was what moved Me Susane when they met in that law office, when they sensed each other and realized they had something in common, or so at least she was convinced.

Rudy foolishly objected to the idea of love founded on a shared background, a shared rank.

"What difference does it make," she would answer, amused, in the early days of their relationship, "that we were drawn together because we were the only ones who came from where we came from? Does that diminish our love in any way?"

She didn't say to Rudy: Besides, what does love matter? Isn't it enough to get along, to talk, to like being together?

She didn't say that because Rudy wanted love in the absolute sense.

How tiring sometimes!

I'm very fond of you, Rudy, Me Susane had never said to him, and you may find those words disappointing but that's as far as my capacity to love will go. So, since I can't manage to love more than that, since I myself don't believe in burning love and since in any case I'm put off by the obligations that come with that sort of love, let's be close companions, let our love be a quiet and virile one.

But Rudy was a sentimental man.

They lived together for three or four years in an old apartment of the Saint-Michel neighborhood, conjointly setting out for the office every morning, and then a relieved Me Susane agreed to Rudy's request for a temporary separation, a request or a plea that he expressed with such sadness that she couldn't bring herself (she was very fond of him!) to display a mere middling grief or, God forbid, an elation at the prospect of being alone at last.

She wept with him, dry, false sobs, thinking it would be helpful since he wanted to leave and thought he was dealing her a crushing blow and bitterly reproached himself for what he assumed was Me Susane's anguish.

She squeezed out a few tears, even as her real heart was pounding with joy.

But she still felt guilty toward Rudy, since she'd deceived him without really wanting to, though without trying not to, and she'd given him every reason to believe she loved him as he defined it.

And when Rudy, heartbroken to realize that he no longer loved Me Susane with the passion he once felt, that he was beginning to see serious failings in her and no doubt took umbrage at the loyal affection she'd shown him instead of the overpowering love he'd offered her, when Rudy announced, choosing his words with the utmost care, that he'd been considering going away, she lied to him again with her tears and her sorrowful words, sparing his feelings, she thought, since he'd shouldered the role of the sensitive one.

In all her time with Rudy, Me Susane never stopped feeling she owed him: he'd given his all, she'd given far less in return.

Still quietly rumbling in her consciousness was the thought that Rudy should have understood who she was and how she loved, that she'd made concessions to his view of love that he would never have made, that he would indignantly have refused to make, to Me Susane's own theory of what a couple should be.

But she rarely thought of all that now.

She was always glad to see Rudy, her oldest friend, the most trustworthy, in truth the only one she sometimes dared to confide in.

Her eagerness to tell him about the Principaux couple kept her on edge as, a little sadly, he told her a few funny stories about his seven-year-old daughter.

He told her those stories because he knew Me Susane had an affection for the little girl.

He told her those stories with no great pleasure, told them only to entertain Me Susane, as he did each time they met.

After their breakup Rudy had met a solicitor's clerk, they married, conceived Lila, then divorced.

At that Rudy felt an incurable bitterness.

Once again Love had betrayed him, Me Susane secretly told herself.

Rudy had Lila every other week, and now and then he entrusted her for a night to Monsieur and Madame Susane, who came to pick up the child in Bordeaux, took her to La Réole, then brought her back to her father the next day.

Me Susane had thrown out the idea of that plan one day when Rudy was complaining he couldn't look after Lila certain evenings, when he had to stay at the office past midnight.

"My parents could watch her from time to time, if that helps," Me Susane had spontaneously offered, knowing the fondness her parents had always felt for Rudy, their sadness when he left her, their wistful delight when they heard Rudy had had a child.

"It should be yours," Madame Susane had said, and Me Susane, feeling as close as she did to Rudy, answered with a little laugh:

"Well, as a matter of fact, it kind of is!"

This arrangement pleased everyone, particularly the child, thought Me Susane, because Lila found in La Réole, in the Susanes' friendly, loyal, unshakable household, a consistency of moods, habits, and schedules that she rarely experienced with her father, or, quite clearly, with her solicitor's clerk mother, who had poisoned Rudy's character and was, he said, utterly and irremediably unhinged.

Me Susane confessed to herself that she felt a vague friendship for that woman who'd managed to disentangle herself from burning love.

Rudy hadn't learned his lesson.

To his mind he'd been robbed, he was never in the wrong.

He was, he proclaimed, still looking for the woman who could appreciate the gift he made of himself when he loved, just as he could recognize such beneficence, and return it.

Still, it seemed to Me Susane that a certain fire had gone out of Rudy, that he no longer felt quite so impatient to fall in love, nor so excited when he thought he had, that he was forcing himself a little to feel burning emotions.

She was always compassionate in her criticisms.

Wasn't he, deep down, her only real friend?

They were growing old together, in one way or another.

Rudy was lean and lanky, all bones and tendons, Me Susane was wide and imposing, a majestic tower.

They'd once made, in the words of Madame Susane, who found it difficult to get over their parting, "a strange but magnificent couple."

Once Rudy completed his account of Lila's little doings, Me Susane hurried to tell him she was having a spat with her parents.

Painfully apprehensive, she even told him she'd blocked her mother's number.

"This isn't the time," she said, "to be asking them to look after Lila."

Rudy stared at her in incomprehension.

"You mean you've broken off with them?"

Nettled, she exclaimed that that's not what it was at all.

Then, suddenly, an idea:

"You remember my housekeeper, Sharon? She could look after Lila, I'll bet she'd say yes."

"But," said Rudy, "you've broken off with your parents?"

He suddenly seemed so disturbed, so disoriented that Me Susane nearly gave him a sharp answer.

Very softly, she said:

"You know, they were the ones who decided to say adieu to me, or rather my father was."

She let out a little laugh, then continued:

"He'll only agree to see me or talk to me if I tell him I was victimized by a certain young man thirty-two years ago. He doesn't

know anything, he doesn't see anything, his imagination is pitiful. And he insists that I was . . . that I was tricked and defiled.
It's absurd, it's obscene, and I have to do battle with my own
father to stop him from transforming my memory, from remak-
ing it to fit the things he's dreamt up! Why should he be so ada-
mant that I was abused? What would he get from that, tell me,
exacting my confession after so many years?"

Me Susane laughed again, a little too loudly to her own ear.

O my impetuous heart, be still, don't reveal yourself!

"Your confession? What confession?" asked Rudy, aghast.

"I never said anything about a confession," she said firmly.

"Yes you did, you used that very word, 'confession.' You were
laughing, but I heard you clearly."

Just then the waitress came to take their order and M^e
Susane, relieved, limp, pretended to be trying to choose between various dishes to draw out the interval after which it
no longer seems quite natural to resume the conversation
where it was interrupted, just as you can scarcely imagine the
possibility, she told herself, of plunging back into the same
bad dream once some external contingency has delivered you
from it.

And indeed, when the waitress was gone Rudy went back
to the subject of Lila, the joys that little girl brought him but
especially the difficulties of taking care of her, and when M^e
Susane again suggested that Sharon look after Lila, Rudy
perked up, interested, enthusiastic, as if he'd forgotten anything else Me Susane had been saying.

She was glad.

"Sharon sometimes works late at my place, she could keep Lila with her, she'd be very happy to earn a little more money," she said, repeating herself, babbling in relief.

"Yes, that's a fine idea."

Rudy smiled at her, full of gratitude.

He didn't know, she mused, how much he loved her, how much he needed her—poor, poor Rudy!

Abruptly changing the subject, she asked him:

"What do you know about the Principaux family?"

"Well," Rudy answered after a pause, "that's that woman who killed her children, right?"

"Yes, but do you know any other people named Principaux?"

Rudy pondered, shook his head.

"No, I can't think of any. Why?"

"There's a certain Madame Principaux who's exploiting Sharon, it's shameful."

Me Susane's voice had suddenly dropped to a conspiratorial hiss, so quiet that Rudy had to bend his long upper body over the table to hear.

"It's immoral, how she forces Sharon to work, she takes advantage of her vulnerability to pay her whenever she feels like it, she punishes her for trifles, that's right, can you imagine, she dares to judge and punish a grown woman, in short she's as good as made Sharon her slave."

"I see," said Rudy. "And what do you mean to do about it? Report her?"

"I can't do that, I'm not employing Sharon legally either, she doesn't have her papers, not yet, I'm working on that, you know. But you understand, the idea of this Principaux woman taking advantage of the situation, I just can't tolerate it."

As if smacked by the tone of Me Susane's voice, Rudy pulled back, retracted his telescoping torso, slumped dubiously in his chair.

"You never told me Sharon wasn't legal . . ."

"She will be soon, that's not the issue. Don't worry, she'll take care of Lila better than any licensed nanny."

Me Susane didn't feel like she was lying to Rudy, although for one thing she knew she wouldn't be resolving Sharon's case anytime soon and for another she had no precise notion of how Sharon was with children.

She knew all the same.

It had come as a hard blow to Me Susane's heart when she ran into Sharon at the shopping center and Sharon pretended not to recognize her: Sharon didn't want to introduce her children, didn't want to grant the kind of woman Me Susane was the honor of making those two admirable little human beings' acquaintance.

She bustled off, her arms laid over her boy's and girl's delicate shoulders, protecting their purity.

From the start, Me Susane had the feeling that Sharon saw her as a dimly, profoundly corrupted woman—a swamp.

And Me Susane hated that about Sharon.

Me Susane felt as blameless of what Sharon's crude intuition was accusing her of as the two gracious, friendly, subtle children on whose shoulders Sharon had made a great show of laying her shielding, puritanical arms.

It was those arms, Me Susane thought angrily, it was the edifying weight of those arms that had denatured the children's innocent hearts.

What would they think of Me Susane when they did finally meet her, as they were bound to one day, and remembered, perhaps, running into that woman in the shopping center?

Would they remember that precisely because their mother, by means of her suddenly heavy, urgent arms on their shoulders, had spared them any supposedly dangerous contact with Me Susane, *had removed them from her toxic orbit?*

Sometimes she hated Sharon, who, it seemed, had privately put Me Susane on trial, had found her guilty, and had pronounced a harsh sentence without the accused having the slightest idea of the wrong she had done.

She senses something about me, but what can it be?

She sees me as unclean, but my God, what did I ever do that could sully me enough for Sharon to smell it (emanating from my skin, from my hair, maybe from my eyes) and so forever after look on me with a loathing full of fear and repugnance?

Oh yes, Me Susane sometimes felt a genuine hatred for Sharon, for being, by that young woman, so unjustly assessed.

Only a heroic sense of professional honor stopped her from dropping the whole thing, showing Sharon the door, shredding the Sharon family file, and forgetting those people once and for all.

But the anger she showed Rudy was sincere: the thought of a Principaux or anyone else hurting Sharon plunged her into a rage she'd never felt for herself.

. . .

She reached one hand toward Rudy, he laid it in his.

They were friends forever.

"I want justice for Sharon," she murmured to him, "and Marlyne as well."

But I don't like them!

How I don't like them!

Later, after the waitress brought them their steak tartare, Me Susane told Rudy of the feast Sharon had offered her, the joy she'd found in those dishes.

She immediately regretted it, like the airing of an inner life, a private self that even Rudy, her one true friend, did not need to know about.

But he had no reaction to her story.

He couldn't understand what it meant or why it mattered, Me Susane thought, relieved, and he was bored by cooking and recipes.

"Incidentally," he said over the post-dinner coffee, "you never explained what your father is trying to make you say. Is he wrong, or do you not want to tell what he knows? What does he know, for that matter? What exactly is all this about?"

"He doesn't know anything," Me Susane answered forcefully. "He's just dreaming. His mind comes up with these clichéd little images, and then he inflates them with all the things he sees on TV. He thinks it's his fatherly duty to be convinced of the worst, even when he has no trace of evidence."

"So," said Rudy, "what you mysteriously call 'the worst' never happened?"

"No," Me Susane said firmly. "Only the best."

. . .

Me Susane knew that if it was up to Sharon she would never say a word about the "two other ladies" she worked for.

Me Susane didn't bring it up with her.

She lavished her praise on the meal of enchantment and remorse, understanding that it was Sharon's way of asking forgiveness for her lie by omission.

But very likely Sharon went right on going to those other ladies' houses, and Me Susane didn't hold it against her, now that she knew and Sharon knew she knew.

Not for a moment did Me Susane think of cutting the salary she paid Sharon on the pretext that her housekeeper had the habit of slipping out for a few hours, since Sharon still left the apartment as spotless as ever.

She only asked her one question, in a voice as casual as she could make it:

"This Madame Principaux, Sharon, what's her address? And Madame Pujol," she added quickly, "where does she live?"

How utterly she did not care about Madame Pujol!

Even Madame Pujol's misdeeds!

She believed she could more easily forgive the basest abuse of her housekeeper by Madame Pujol than the pettiest meanness of a Madame Principaux.

But she didn't want Sharon to grasp that obsession.

"I'd rather write it down," Sharon murmured.

She looked away, her proud little head perched high atop her frail neck, her tiny ears not quite able to hold back her long, straight, flowing hair, and Sharon made the gesture that

Me Susane loved to catch her in: her weary fingernails slicing through the locks to put them back in their place, behind those exquisite ears, and the persistent trace of that gesture, like furrows in black soil.

Me Susane and Sharon were standing in the kitchen.

The cold sun gently lit the four gleaming little cast-iron stewpots that Me Susane had decided to set very visibly on a shelf.

Sharon tore off a piece of paper towel, and Me Susane ran to her purse for a pen.

Later, when Sharon had gone, Me Susane opened the scrap of paper, which Sharon had folded in six: "Princip 27 place pey berland cod 5632 Puj 30 rue rosa bonheur."

The snow fell every night, melted in the morning, then the cold came back and froze the dirty water on the pavement.

A muffled lethargy fell over Bordeaux, every intention, it seemed, suspended.

Me Susane was still waiting for word from Marlyne Principaux, whom she already considered, illegitimately, incautiously, her client.

With difficulty, with tiny skidding steps, she walked to 27 Place Pey-Berland in the reserved, chaste light of an implacable winter day.

"It's dangerous riding your bicycle on the ice," she'd told Sharon, "I'd rather you not come to work for the time being."

Sharon had answered exactly as Me Susane thought she

would answer, and in the tone Me Susane had foreseen, sharp and detached, angry and hurt.

"I'll come, it's not a problem."

"Did the other ladies not say anything to you? They didn't tell you not to ride your bike for the moment?"

"I don't talk with the other ladies," Sharon murmured, "I don't meddle in their lives and they don't meddle in mine."

"When, Sharon, are you going to bring me your marriage certificate?" Me Susane then asked, brusquely.

How she was struggling to choke back her anger at the two other ladies!

Fearing that Sharon might think her sharp tone was meant for her, she very gently added:

"I told you, I need it for your file. If you think you can come up with it . . ."

"Yes," said Sharon, irritated, "I just need some time to look for it, you see?"

She raised her eyebrows, turned her back, overtly, regally, doing her best to stay patient with Me Susane—hadn't they already talked about that marriage certificate business?

"Well, I have to put together the file," Me Susane mumbled, almost begging her forgiveness.

"Yes, yes, of course," said Sharon, just as if she were patting Me Susane on the arm to calm her down.

And then there was no room for doubt, thought Me Susane, shocked: unmistakably, Sharon was patronizing her.

She stood still for a few seconds at number 27's tall olive-green porte cochere, her booted feet planted far apart on the slippery pavement, forcefully belted in her big gray wool coat—gray too was her short, thick hair, once exceedingly long, many-tinged, and proud.

As a child, Me Susane had such hair, adorned herself with it, devoted long hours to it, frivolous, obsessive, vain hours!

Her parents, and especially her father, basked in the glory of that hair.

Madame Susane's was nowhere near so beautiful.

Monsieur Susane's mind was always full of illusions on that score: perhaps his daughter wasn't "pretty as a picture," but she was nonetheless endowed with a mane so profuse, shimmering, enigmatic, and perfumed that it vicariously made him feel rich, and maybe not even vicariously, Me Susane sometimes thought.

She avoided remembering, so much did the memory sadden her, that her father had shown genuine despair when she cut her hair, then had long given her the cold shoulder, as if his own locks had been brutally amputated, he who had nothing to be proud of—as if someone had set out to diminish and humiliate him, he who possessed nothing to be proud of apart from his daughter's luxuriant hair.

Now Me Susane's hair was short, gray, and bushy, sometimes bristling when she unthinkingly combed it with too vigorous a hand.

"You spend one afternoon with those people and then you cut your hair!" an inconsolable Monsieur Susane had exclaimed.

"So what?" sighed Me Susane, with all the weight of her ten years, her tone vaguely menacing. "What can you possibly care? It was on my head, not yours!"

Monsieur Susane had retreated, unused to combat, to raised voices, by nature hating dissent and at the same time so fond of his daughter that he couldn't imagine ever going against her, for fear she might think he loved her less.

But he'd loved her so proudly and wholeheartedly when she bore that glinting, amber-chestnut splendor above her little face, which was in every other way ordinary—did he, afterward, love her resentfully, with a slight distance, as if Me Susane had immolated what he loved most about her, or more precisely the one aspect of her physique that didn't put Monsieur Susane off?

Because she knew, from her childhood on, that she wasn't pretty.

She knew, without anyone saying so outright, that the irreparable absence of prettiness in a cherished little girl can only be a cruel disappointment for her parents.

She also knew that those parents have a tendency, paradoxical but customary, unavoidable and therefore forgivable, to hold it against the little girl for not being pretty instead of blaming their own flaws, which, numerous, multiplied in the act of reproduction, appear flagrantly and lamentably in the child's face and body.

Me Susane had always known that!

As a child, she'd accepted her broad, full face, without planes or cheekbones, her narrow brow, her over-round eyes, with a determination all the more cheerful in that she thought she might thereby free her parents from their disappointment (at not having given birth to a "little princess," as Madame Susane put it when she spoke of certain sweet-faced little girls).

And she succeeded, yes!

Aided by her magnificent hair, the privilege of brushing which Monsieur and Madame Susane gently fought over when she was little, which she later tended to herself, with an attention proportional to the place that hair occupied in her parents' life—a devoted attention, obsessive, consuming, but which was no burden for her because she was doing it for them, as much to please them as to earn their forgiveness (successfully!) for her incontestable lack of beauty, or to make them forget it.

Still, as a girl, Me Susane did have one great asset: she was tall, and her parents weren't.

Compared to theirs her height was even miraculous, mysterious, almost terrifying.

That advantage turned into a flaw when Me Susane became an ample young lady.

She'd filled out all over, immoderately.

She'd become a strange colossus, nothing graceful or endearing about her, rather she radiated a hard and disconcerting power, an obtuse solidity that, the day she turned fifteen, had brought this remark, half joking, half fuming, to Monsieur Susane's lips:

"I thought I had a daughter, and it turns out I have a strapping son!"

Me Susane had been wearing her hair short for five years by then.

Monsieur Susane had never quite gotten over it.

"She's too fat," he sometimes whispered to Madame Susane, thinking his daughter couldn't hear. "She's huge, she's gigantic, she looks like a man!"

And Me Susane, devastated by those words, resolved to boldly hold her shorn head high.

She swore, vaguely but firmly, that she would never again have long hair.

She was proud, though gravely hurt.

But, knowing she was hurt, she felt no shame about it.

She punched in the code Sharon had given her.

She climbed the fine stone staircase to the third floor and, fumblingly following Sharon's imprecise directions, rang at a door that opened not onto the vast landing with pale stone walls but onto an isolated corner of that landing—like a service door, she thought, surprised, because Sharon had given her the impression there was no other entrance to Madame Principaux's apartment.

She waited, rang again.

An explosion of light suddenly left her half-blind.

A bright, pale flame, a white-hot iron bar in front of her eyes.

Staggering, Me Susane slumped with one shoulder against the door just as it opened.

Her right eye was on fire—*oh Mother, save me!*

She also thought: I'm drowning, I'm sinking into hard, dirty water, why don't you save me, why am I having to fight you and your incomprehensible insistence on keeping my head in the . . .

Me Susane stumbled through the doorway.

She thought she felt her face collide with someone's chest.

"My eyes hurt," she murmured.

"Hey now!"

The voice was surprised but calm, phlegmatically startled.

Two arms, fleshy, forceful, pushed Me Susane's head away and then slipped under her arms, pulling up the gray overcoat's woolly sleeves, to stop her from falling, from fainting.

Gray is the beautiful alpaca overcoat I'm still paying installments on, and gray is my hair, which is no longer a mane and won't give me away to the Principaux woman's memory, any more than my face, which has been changed by the years—but my eyes, oh God . . .

Would that Principaux woman remember Me Susane by her gaze?

"Everything's all right, it's going to be fine, everything's all right," the woman who opened the door was saying.

Me Susane stood up straight, smoothed her rebellious hair.

She was taken aback to hear a slight accent in that woman's voice.

"Excuse me," she mumbled, "yes, I'm better now, I'm sorry."

"It's no problem, no problem at all."

She was even taller than Me Susane, dressed in a tracksuit, a young woman with braided hair bound up in a chignon atop her head.

"Are you Madame Principaux?"

"Oh no!"

She was smiling, amused that anyone might think such a thing.

"And," Me Susane struggled to say, "is Madame Principaux in?"

"Yes. But you won't be able to see her."

"Oh?"

"Madame Principaux doesn't see anyone."

"You work here?"

"Yes. I've got to be going now, I have things to do."

"Tell her I came by!" Me Susane cried.

"And you are?"

Me Susane hesitated, flustered.

Who was she to the Principaux woman?

"Well, tell her I'm the daughter of Madame Susane, the ironing lady."

Do those people remember our name? her mother had hissed.

Who was Me Susane to all the Principauxs?

And who were those various Principauxs to each other?

"The ironing lady from La Réole," she rushed to say before the door could close, "I'm her daughter, Madame Principaux will understand."

A hint of wariness appeared on the woman's vigilant face.

Me Susane sensed she was coming off as strange, vaguely worrisome.

And, as if liberated, she let out a little laugh.

She thought she could hear the muscles of her frozen cheeks creaking as they stretched.

"The Principauxs chose me, each in their own way, tell her that too, and tell her also how . . . how grateful I am!"

"Very well."

That purple-haired young woman exhaled a cold, unfriendly, untrusting breath, as if, thought Madame Susane, she were instinctively taking the Principaux woman's side, shielding her, determined to spare her any anxiety.

Me Susane understood that the Principaux woman would not, and in a way absolutely not, be informed of her visit.

A snicker escaped her.

And she repeated that bitter little laugh, that resentful belch, not without a bilious pleasure, since the Principaux woman was not going to show herself, would never show herself.

Suddenly free, her heart swelled with boldness.

"Your madame certainly has a lot of employees!" she exclaimed. "There's Sharon, there's you, and who else, and for what kind of money, hm? Tell her that won't go on much longer! Tell her I know everything!"

She forced herself to transform that acrimonious burp into a laugh, she laughed uproariously, for several seconds, before the closed door.

Is that me acting this way?

How strange! she mused, at the same time.

She wasn't far from impressed by this version of Me Susane.

When she found the letter from Marlyne Principaux, she gently laid it down unopened on her desk.

She dealt with her client who wanted to change his name, even though it was a beautiful name, well-known, enviable from many points of view.

Her client claimed it was the name of a slave trader.

Me Susane could find no confirmation of that, no matter how she searched.

But the man was sure of it.

He was implacable, vengeful, he was undaunted, and his family had furiously rejected him.

Me Susane treated him with cautious understanding.

She was working to come up with damning evidence on the ancestor, so far unsuccessfully, despite all the long hours she'd spent digging into that wine merchant's life.

That morning a very fine snow hung a curtain over the office windows, an opacity made for illusions, for words mumbled to oneself, for thoughts dwelled on in an inspired, truculent, retaliatory mood.

Me Susane knew that, she knew to be wary of her penchant for casting blame.

And so it was only slowly, with deep detachment, that she opened Marlyne Principaux's letter.

How she disliked that woman!

But how grateful that she'd accepted Me Susane as her lawyer, she who'd never pleaded a case in criminal court, never proven that she could save a living soul!

She immediately thought of calling her parents, then, remembering that this wasn't the time, and that in any case they would show only a cold disgust at the Principaux case, she sadly closed the door on her heartfelt longing to win their respect.

In her office with its snow-veiled windows, perfectly alone and insignificant, she dived into her investigation, already sensing it would go nowhere, of the slave-trading wine merchant.

All the same, she felt overjoyed, excited, frightened, ready even now to do battle—because Marlyne had chosen her, and Me Susane's deepest-buried thoughts flew far from the wine merchant and even farther from that client whose need for a passion had settled on his hated name.

Why, she vaguely wondered, did that intelligent, well-to-do, attractive man, that man who "had everything going for him" as Madame Susane would have said, not have something else to be furious or inflamed about than that name, which was undoubtedly innocent (or at least not conclusively guilty)?

When, a few days later, she set out to see Marlyne Principaux at the jail in Gradignan, her old Twingo wouldn't start, sheepish, wheezy, and hiccupping, the only member of its age group in the bays of the Tourny parking lot.

Anxious, Me Susane ended up on the bus.

She feared she might be unacceptably late.

She made the trip standing, sweating in her long overcoat.

Her scalp tingled, as if it needed to be washed, scraped, scoured.

She blankly raised her hand to her head, combed her hair with her trembling fingers.

At her feet sat a big, beautiful satchel of tanned leather, empty but heavy all the same.

Me Susane had nothing to put in it.

The old leather, the brass hardware, the many zippered pockets: all that fine workmanship was a burden to transport.

Me Susane had told herself she couldn't meet her client for the first time carrying only her purse, she would feel too casual, unserious.

And so she armed herself with this satchel, which her parents had given her after she'd earned her degree, going so far as to have it specially made by a leather craftsman they knew in the Gers, where they sometimes liked to go camping.

It was a lawyer's satchel from another age, a satchel for the

Susanes' dream lawyer, a man of boundless energy, brawny, athletic, a chain-smoking dynamo, lovably disorganized but adept at filing anything that had to be filed in the multiple compartments of that elegant expanding satchel, a sort of stylish doctor, a doctor of the abstract, who never left home without his intellectual instruments.

So minutely did Me Susane study the Marlyne Principaux who walked into the visiting room that at first she didn't see her.

She blinked, extended a tentative hand toward the woman.

For the first few seconds she registered only pieces of a face, like bits of a painting neatly cut up into three or four fragments.

She had a sense of the forehead, smooth, rather low, a thick growth of dull blond hair, then the short nose, slightly upturned, then the mouth, big, wide, pale, with limp, trembling lips.

She didn't see her eyes.

Searching but selective, her gaze avoided them.

She extended a tentative hand and felt the other woman's slip into hers even more limply, then at once pull away—reticent, uncomfortable, modest?

Forcing herself to pull back her lips to put a friendly expression on her face, Me Susane then turned her eyes to Marlyne's.

Glassy, oddly unstill, dull green, grayish—a pond stirred by falling rain, Me Susane thought immediately.

How that woman repelled her!

Marlyne Principaux was neither tall nor short.

Madame Susane, thought Me Susane, would have called Marlyne sturdy: thick, straight legs in faded black jeans, broad, round shoulders under the Université de la Sorbonne sweat-shirt, short-fingered hands, hardworking, square.

A heartiness, a full-bodied, muscular good health that troubled Me Susane.

There was no sign of desolation about her.

But why should a gaunt body, a drawn face, or an unwhole-some corpulence be the only possible incarnations of torment, of a grieving soul, a guilty heart?

Was there, in this little room, a grieving soul, a guilty heart?

How to know?

In spite of her figure, plump and firm, hard and rounded, Marlyne Principaux struck Me Susane as a discreet and unimposing person.

Quick and silent, she sank onto the chair.

She kept her industrious hands tightly clasped on her thighs, hunched her back, pressed her knees together.

She had a ponytail like a little girl's, thought Me Susane: a bright pink scrunchie bound her dull yellow hair.

But how cold her eyes were!

Or tired, worried, and that made them seem cold?

How to know?

Slightly intimidated, Me Susane introduced herself.

Marlyne nodded absently, politely, her vague gaze fixed on Me Susane's shoulder.

She regularly raised her right hand to tuck back a lock of hair that hadn't moved, trapped as it was by the scrunchie, but her hand stayed raised and after a moment came the sound of her fingers scratching the delicate skin between her hairline and the top of her ear.

With her permission, Me Susane recorded their conversation.

Me Susane asked many questions, and Marlyne answered them with no show of reluctance but as briefly as possible, such that it would later seem to Me Susane that she'd done more talking than Marlyne.

She would be slightly annoyed with herself, and a little embarrassed as well, that she might have come across as too talkative.

"But yes, but I'm happy here but everyone's nice to me now. But it was different at first but I can understand that but I don't blame anyone but now they accept me as I am, with my act, and even if it's hard for some of the women around me but they accept me now, yes. But we're not here to like each other. But the wardens treat me well too, yes. But I'm fine. But nothing's troubling me, yes. But the food's very good, I always clean my plate. But sometimes a little cold, yes, but you know, before, but I often ate cold food, but children can easily disturb your meals [embarrassed, almost frightened little laugh]. But right now I wouldn't like to be anywhere other than this jail. But I don't have a house of my own anymore, but that's fine with me. But, no, our house in Le Bouscat, but I didn't like it, but I came to hate it. But I prefer my cell and my own little bed. But no, because I put on my headphones, but I reread the writers I so used to love, but I don't hear anything, but the others can watch TV, but I don't hear anything, but I'm happy here, the atmosphere's nice. But a little space like that, just for me, but the very precise little place for my bed, but the nest I've made for myself, but I never had one so nice. But it's a real home sweet home [hesitant little laugh]. But my act can't get in. But it's there, in the atmosphere of the cell, since the others think about it, but the emanations of their thoughts never get through the walls of my dear little lair. But I don't need anything, thanks. But something to eat, to drink? But no but no, I'm a frugal person you know and simplicity, even austerity where food is concerned but that suits me perfectly, but I'd even say I quite like it, yes. But there's no one depending on me. But I don't have to think about pleasing anyone. But Monsieur Principaux always enjoyed a good meal. But yes, but he loved to eat, but he loved richness, life, tradition, but just eating without thinking of anything other than pleasure and he expected me to answer that love, but he implicitly asked me for richness, life, tradition, and simple pleasure. But it was hard, yes. But I had to think of the children, I had to keep track of their growth. But their growth had to be right in every way. But I couldn't handle it. But I ate too much but I showed it whereas Monsieur Principaux stayed skinny even though he ate far too much. Fat, life, good cheer, but saints eat all they like and it never shows. But Monsieur Principaux is a saint, yes. But a very trivial curse hung over my little body, which kept getting heavier even as Monsieur Principaux's got thinner, leaner, more muscular. But there's no doubt about it, Monsieur Principaux is a saint. But me, I balloon in direct proportion to my inadequacy. But I'd like to spend the rest of my life here, yes. But could I ask you for one thing, and then after that nothing ever again? But could Monsieur Principaux stop visiting, but could they take away his right to come see me? But it's very painful for me, yes. But I'd like never to see him again. But is that possible? But I'm his wife, but he's quite aware of that. But he thinks it's his duty to come visit me and his right and that alone would be enough to bring him here even though I won't talk to him. But I never say anything to Monsieur Principaux anymore. But I'm ashamed before him. But I hate him too, and that makes me more ashamed. But I can't sort it out. But I pity him, but I hate him, but I'm ashamed before him as before God. But no, I'm not a believer. But it's an image. But I'm ashamed before him as before God. But I'm glad God is suffering as I suffer. But he's far better than me, of course. But he's suffering, apparently, but although. But ask him if he misses the children. But I don't think he does, but I think that, alone in his house in Le Bouscat, he's suffering and whimpering but he's enjoying being alone and he doesn't miss the children's real presence in any way. But they quickly got on his nerves, you know. But he doesn't like playing with kids or particularly talking to them, but the often tedious reality of daily life with young children exasperated him, but he sometimes shouted at us: Leave me alone, will you! Even though our boys hardly came near him, they could smell hostility and wariness all around Monsieur Principaux's body, and that kept them at a distance, it made them timid even as they yearned for contact with their papa. But they galloped around Monsieur Principaux, making sure to keep out of that hostility's range. But they didn't touch him. But they shouted: Papa, Papa! as they ran around two or three meters away from Monsieur Principaux. But he liked being a father, but all the same, yes. But he said: I'd like a great big family, five, six, seven children! But the very concrete presence of the children in his house always startled him. What are those little intruders doing here? But I think I'm translating Monsieur Principaux's sentiments fairly well. But he liked being a father, yes, as a status. But I'm ashamed before him, but I never want to talk to him again. But his still wanting to visit me, but to understand me and support me, but all that makes me hate him. But why doesn't he push me away in horror? But he's been given his freedom, yes. But martyred children, but a wife to defend in spite of everything, but Monsieur Principaux is a hero, along with a saint. But he's there in our living room, but he's there all alone and finally at peace, but he's sipping his evening scotch, but he's suffering, but he's happy, but he's thinking about my trial, about the newspaper articles, but he's happy, but he takes a sip, but he's thinking of the things he's going to say, but he suffers with a suffering that brings him fulfillment and relief, but he's happy, but he has no obligations toward anyone. But I understand him. But I don't hate him for that but I hate him for the hypocrisy of his pose. But now he's so proud of himself for getting me the best defense possible. But I never asked him for anything. But no! But I don't want to have the best defense possible, but I don't want to be defended at all. But I'm happy here. But I'd like to have nothing more to do with Monsieur Principaux, but I know it's not possible, but he'll always be the father of the children who by my act . . . But I don't want to be defended. But I performed my act, but I knew I wouldn't be beheaded. But that act, but I did it. But I can't be sorry for it, but that would be indecent. But it's done, I did it. Monsieur Principaux? But I'm certain he doesn't miss the children. But he's been set free, but he's suffering, he's happy. But he's mourning sincerely, but he's truly suffering, yes. But he's been set free. But if I could, thanks to you, be sure I never came face-to-face with him in the visiting room. But is that possible, being his wife? But my hatred of him, but I don't think he should have to find out how deep it runs. But please, but see to it that he won't come visit me anymore, but I beg of you see to it also that he doesn't know this is coming from me, but it wouldn't be good for him to learn the depths of my hatred, but I have no wish to hurt his feelings. But it's impossible, but I understand, but you can't lie for me, but I understand. But then I'll tell him myself to stop visiting. But the poor man! But I won't say anything against him, but I don't have the spiritual permission. But he's suffering, but he's happy, he's sipping his . . . But I don't remember what it was, scotch, cognac, gin, but I don't recall. But he's happy, alone in our house, but I can see him clearly, he . . . But he answers emails from people who pity him, but he plays the brave man hiding his tears, but no tear ever dampened so much as the rims of his eyes. But Monsieur Principaux is strong, in his saintliness. But I won't say anything against him, but I can't do that. But who are the victims of the act? But not me, surely. But the children and him, yes. But he's happy, in his solitude. But he often yelled at us: Leave me alone! Leave me in peace for one moment! But we took great care to get close to him only if we sensed that his body was relaxed and his mind ready to receive the reminder that we existed. But we left him alone, but I rigorously made sure of that and the children obeyed me. But why did he yell like that? Leave me alone! But I was always afraid. But of noise, but of disorder, but of irritations.

"But do I miss the children? But I don't know. But I'd rather not talk about it. But it wouldn't be right. But I performed my act, I performed my act. But it wouldn't be decent to talk about my feelings. But I took their lives. But I see them when I'm asleep, but they're in all my dreams. But I wouldn't say I sob in my sleep, even if I do. But it's obscene to say it. But I don't miss them, no. But I've brought them back inside me, they're tiny, in my brain. But in my belly they were all three big babies, but they were born after term, but beautiful children, heavy and long. But my God, how substantial they were! But now they're teeny-tiny in my brain. But it doesn't torment me that they're not actually there anymore, but beside me. But I robbed them of their lives, but they didn't want to die. But Jason resisted. But I had to grapple with him, but it wasn't the angels who carried him off, but it was me, but his loving mother. But how I loved my oldest son! But I hadn't expected him to put up a fight, I thought his mother's will would silence his will to survive. But we wrestled. But I think he cried out, or tried to, but I'm not sure anymore. But I closed my eyes. But yes, I closed my eyes. But his gaze just when he . . . but when he realized he was dying, but I didn't see it, I don't think. But John, on the other hand, John didn't struggle, but I don't believe he did. But I gently pushed him down into the water but his muscles relaxed almost immediately, like when I used to massage him in the evening after story time, but he went limp but tender but accepting. But I think so, but yes. But he was such a docile little boy, but so trusting, but so eager to be good. But he consented to the act, yes. But he didn't oppose his mama, but he always liked to make her happy. But his mama, but that was me, but I had to see my act through, but John helped me and it wasn't hard. But I helped him too. But I talked to him through the whole thing, yes, but I whispered loving words in his ear. But oh, I don't remember exactly. But the usual words: 'my darling,' 'my sweetheart,' 'my little one,' but the endearments I used more than their real names when I talked to them. But that irritated Monsieur Principaux. But he thought it was affected, but ridiculous, but childish. I mean *because* he thought it was affected, ridiculous, childish. But he didn't like it, no. But he always called them by their names. But as for Julia, my baby . . . But I was nursing her, she took my breast with joy but I felt pride and relief, but gratitude too. But, no not but, *because* I felt terribly hurt when she used to take the breast half-heartedly or worse yet refused it altogether. But it was my duty to still be nursing my baby after six months, but I couldn't do otherwise, but you understand, yes, but I'd nursed her brothers for twenty-four, but that was a wonderful thing for them, but they were healthy and handsome, but I had to do the same thing with Julia, who had just as much right as they did to be healthy and pretty, but so she took my breast greedily that day and I felt grateful even as I begged her in advance to forgive me. But I shouldn't say that? Premeditation? But I don't want you to redeem me. But I don't care about the sentence I'll get. But I'm happy in my little nest. But, yes, I'd like you to leave now. But I'm tired. *Because* I'm tired, I mean. But I don't want you telling me how to avoid the worst. But what is the worst? But they're not going to cut my head off. But what is it? But twenty years in jail? But I don't want you to prevent that. But I'm not asking you for anything. But he's the one who made you come here, it was Monsieur Principaux. But I don't want anything, but I'm happy as I am. But leave now, yes, thanks. But thanks, yes [Me Susane, with a firm, friendly movement, grasped Marlyne's shoulders above the little table, through the thick fabric of the sweatshirt she squeezed the contracted muscles of that woman who filled her with terror and loathing and Marlyne Principaux calmed down, stopped talking about ending the meeting or complaining she was tired]. But he would have led them to despise me, but of course. But to laugh at me, you know. But why? But he felt no respect for me. But he laughed at me, yes, then claimed to love me. But he had no real consideration for Marlyne. But I'd disappointed him, yes. But I'm drab. But I'm a boring wife, you know. But I wasn't, I don't think, a boring teacher. But the students liked me, yes, but I think so. But Monsieur Principaux wasn't my student, but there was nothing I could teach him. But he must have thought me such a bore! But he laughed at me, but a bitter laugh. But the joy I found in teaching, but he scorned it, but he thought it was absurd, impossible, but it made him angry, but he said I was deluding myself about my work. But he said: That worthless school of yours, but he also said: You work too hard, but he also said: They're going to kill you. But I thought: If anyone on this earth kills me, but it will be Monsieur Principaux. But I said to myself: My dear students, protect me from the slow murder being forced on me by my life with Monsieur Principaux, I love my students and I don't love Monsieur Principaux. But then I was ashamed. But I couldn't fault my husband for anything. But I used to sing his praises to my mother, to my sisters, but I was ashamed. But I didn't know how to go about getting away from all that. But . . . how happy I was when Jason was born! But I was grateful to Monsieur Principaux, who was, but you already know, but a handsome man, but I'm not a beautiful woman, but Jason turned out to be a magnificent child. But I'm not a beautiful woman, but I'm like you. But, no, but of course. But Monsieur Principaux didn't choose me for my looks, but it was admirable of him to love, but to conquer a woman who could only, but in every way, but disappoint him. But not as a mother. But I was, but he'll tell you, but an excellent mother. But everyone agrees about that. But I don't know who everyone is, but we saw almost no one, but it's true. But what about the other teachers? But didn't they tell you I was a near-perfect mother? But the friends, but Monsieur Principaux's colleagues who came to the house? But didn't they tell you that? But my mother and my sisters, didn't they agree? But you don't know them, but what will they tell you now that they've been turned against me? But it was Monsieur Principaux I wanted to eradicate from my existence but it wasn't possible. But it wasn't possible. But he'd bound me to him. I mean *because* he'd bound me to him, and the only way I could undo that knot, those chains, was by . . . But I couldn't murder Monsieur Principaux, could I [a little laugh, would-be sardonic but frightened, thin, pitiful]? But you can't kill Monsieur Principaux, even in your imagination. But you can't leave Monsieur Principaux, even in your dreams. But yes you can, actually, but in your dreams you can go away, but abandon all that, but Monsieur Principaux, the children, the house, but everything, you know, but that whole life. But in the real world, but no, no, no. But no, no, you understand. But he would have crushed me, but he would have destroyed me, but he would have trained, would have raised the children to hate me. But, no not but, *because* for that he had weapons I knew nothing of. But I don't really know what I'm saying anymore. But I know the main idea but not the fine points, the details. But I don't want to accuse Monsieur Principaux, who, because of me, has found himself in a horrific situation but I'd like you, Maître what was it? Maître Susane, excuse me, but I'd like you to erase from your memory and your recording anything acrimonious I might have said about Monsieur Principaux. But about Gilles, yes, if you like. But I don't have the right to put Gilles on trial [little laugh]. But I don't have the right to incriminate poor Principaux, do I? But the children . . . but the children . . . but where are they now? But they always wanted what Mama wanted, but they were always afraid of displeasing me, but of causing me heartache. But where are they? But I'm afraid Monsieur Principaux's thoughts might draw their poor little souls to him, but sway them to his side, but to . . . but to his wrong way of seeing everything. But it was Monsieur Principaux I should have drowned in his filthy bathwater. Instead I delivered him of a weight, but yes. But that's not what I wanted. But Monsieur Principaux has become a tragic figure, hasn't he? But that's not what I wanted. But he tells me we'll be together again when all this is over. Maître . . . Maître Susane, forgive me, but I'm begging you, tell him I don't want anything more to do with him, now or later. But tell him I hate him. But tell him . . ."

Marlyne then began to tremble with her whole being.

And her lips quivered and her eyelids vibrated, and her right hand tried to contain the shaking of her left while her short, restless, muscular thighs twitched as if she'd just finished some athletic event.

Me Susane stood up, walked around the table, came closer to Marlyne's shuddering body.

She saw herself laying her arm on Marlyne's shoulders, bending her head toward her, murmuring vague words.

She couldn't touch her.

She'd embraced her not long before, she thought.

So what was that about?

She saw her arm reaching out toward Marlyne.

But she clearly felt her arm not moving at all, she could see that as if it was what she wanted to happen but she knew beyond all doubt that it was her, Me Susane, who was standing there cold and mute, petrified and deeply, irrevocably reproachful before the hiccupping flesh of that woman she couldn't bring herself even to fleetingly graze with her hand.

That's no way for Me Susane to behave, she told herself.

She forced herself to raise her arm, she thought she had.

Once again she saw herself embracing Marlyne, patting her back as, even formally, even with disgust, any lawyer would do with her client.

But she couldn't move, her arms hung straight and stiff at her sides, and, she felt it, her face was frozen in a cold, flat look of aversion.

The next day, she was busy transcribing Marlyne's words when Gilles Principaux appeared in her office.

"Cold day!" he exclaimed, rubbing his hands like, she told herself, a character, a recurring television-series part that

Gilles Principaux was condemned to play whether he liked it or not, whether he had any talent for it or not.

In a faintly uneasy voice, his hands rubbing each other mechanically, he repeated:

"Cold day, isn't it?"

He reached out toward Me Susane, his fingers long and thin, pale, but pinker at the knuckles.

Did those hands remind her of anything?

She thought he didn't look well.

She might have told him so, feigning solicitude, unless she merely thought it and imagined herself saying it and pretending to care.

How strange his face was, how disagreeable!

Me Susane had no precise memory of the Caudéran boy's face, however her fevered mind labored to remember, day and night.

Could she, she wondered uneasily, have loved, have admired such a face, could she have wanted to impress that face and bask in the praise of a boy whose features would become the rumpled, indistinct, very common face of Gilles Principaux?

How could she, at such a young age, have guessed that that teenager would turn into a lackluster adult, a man of no particular merit, unworthy of the ten-year-old girl who would throw everything she had into dazzling him and thereby lose the simple love of her father, the spontaneous, unstinting trust of her parents?

Had she not, in that room, offered up everything she had to offer, *everything there was to be ransacked*?

There was nothing calculated in her devotion, nothing cautious.

And that was how the Caudéran boy won her: place your hazy hopes for life in my hands because I'm destined to be an exceptional person. I'll subjugate you, I'll keep you, I'll convince you even if you hesitate. And you'll be happy, looking back you'll be flattered when you discover the man who comes to be in me.

But this Principaux, with his lifeless, shifty eyes, cunning, almost blank!

She offered him a coffee, he dropped into one of the two armchairs facing her desk.

Who was Principaux to her?

Those dull eyes, were those his real eyes or the eyes he used for putting on fronts, for glad-handing, were those his deceiving eyes?

She studied him, looked at him with a furious scrutiny that, she thought, should have alarmed him concerning the old bonds that might have united them.

But he didn't move.

And Me Susane sensed that she stirred no memory in Gilles Principaux, that to him she was simply the inexpensive, convenient tool for a more or less effective defense of his wife.

That man, she sadly concluded, did not recognize her.

"You've met her now, what did she say?" he asked in a voice at once hard and gentle, imperious and silken.

"She gave me an account of the events," said Me Susane curtly.

"But what did she say to you? I wish I could know, she doesn't tell me anything..."

Since Me Susane didn't answer, Principaux launched into his own narration, agitated, clumsily trying to charm, but so distraught that a strand of saliva hung unnoticed from his chin, swaying in time with his words.

"We were happy, I can assure you of that," he proclaimed in an ostentatiously vigorous voice, "happy in a way it's hard to be nowadays. Sometimes, on a Sunday morning, we used to let the three children into our bed, big Jason who was learning to read and was so proud of his progress, little John who listened to his brother, and baby Julia who gurgled with the enthusiasm that always comes after nursing, yes, we were so happy, all five of us, in the little love nest that was our bed. It was, yes, I must say, it was paradise: the two of us and the little ones in that nice warm bed with the rain pattering on the windowpanes. I would read, Marlyne would tell the children stories, babbling and laughing with them, we were happy, yes, at peace, happy and proud that we'd reached our goals. Our goals? Well, to found a big family with nothing forcing us to, quite the reverse. On that point we went radically against our parents' ideas. Marlyne was fine, yes, she was happy. She never stopped talking about the children, she told me she'd 'found herself as a woman'—as a mother, you know. Myself, I wasn't so sure. I will confess that I prefer life without children. I'm not that fond of children's company, it quickly gets old, I never quite understand what I'm doing with them. But those three, Jason John Julia, I loved them enormously! You have to believe me, I loved them with a love I'd never known, tender, tolerant, I'd even say boundless—

yes, there was no limit to my love for them, you understand? I loved to take them in my arms, inhale their scent of fresh or damp grass when they'd been playing outside on a Sunday afternoon, I also loved the simple love they felt for me. Yes, I was their beloved papa, there's no question. We were happy. I believe I was an ideal papa. Because they loved me, and feared me just as much. When they loved me, they'd forgotten all about the troubles of the night before, some foolishness or disobedience we'd punished them for, even some disappointment we'd fallen prey to. I'm sure I don't need to tell you, parents are so easily tortured by our cherished children's violations of the family laws. That's why I wanted them to fear me as much as they loved me. And like well-behaved dogs they could love me and be wary of me at the same time, love me during the day, forgetting the rancors of the night. Every morning I was a new father for them, a virgin father. Yes, I was a loved and loving father, I believe I can say that without immodesty. But a father who would rather never have been one. I would have liked to be a man without offspring. No, I never told Marlyne, no, no. She wanted children, didn't she? She says the opposite now, I don't want to argue with her through you who represent her, I'll go along with everything she says, I won't dispute a word. But allow me simply to observe that various signs, among them some very clear statements on the subject, led me to believe, beyond all doubt, that Marlyne dreamt of a big family. And she was right! Because just the two of us . . . What sense would there have been in our joining together, in our unlikely union, if there were no children? If there were no plan to found a beautiful, exemplary tribe, to create a lineage? What did Marlyne and I have in common? Nothing at all, nothing at all. We never loved each other, I mean sentimentally, totally, romantically. Oh, I love her, yes! I still love the mother of my children, even though... I love my wife, she's my wife and I made a commitment to her, I have duties toward her, she's my wife for better or worse. This is the worse, that's how it is. I love her, I won't abandon her, maybe I even love her more, and more truly, than I did before. My love is sacred, unshakable. No, we weren't madly in love when we first knew each other, when we had the children. The bonds that held us were loose. Now our bond is a tragic one. I love that horrifying Marlyne, I don't quite understand her, but I can't hate her. I love my wife, that's all, whatever sort of person she is. I blame myself for so much! I love her more truly than I did before, yes. She was an ordinary person. She's become a dark heroine. I'm surprised. I never imagined her like that. I'm surprised. She's strange. Horrifying, yes. But I thought she was like anyone else, and I was wrong. I blame myself for so much! I should have insisted she go back to work after Jason was born. I didn't, I thought she... I thought she was happy, glad to be out of it. I didn't like her school in Pauillac. Her? Yes, probably, at least she said she did. But was it a good place for her, I'm not sure it was. The students were very middling, her colleagues burnt-out or sarcastic or defeated, and then there was that long drive from Bordeaux... She claims I forbade her to go back to work. Who was I to forbid her anything? She was an independent, intelligent woman, perfectly capable of weighing her opinions and her husband's on an honest scale. She could make whatever decisions she thought best, I wouldn't have objected. I never yelled at Marlyne, not once. I never scolded her, humiliated her, ridiculed her. I was not the head of our good little team. We were equal partners in the nonprofit organization that was our family. But I can only fault myself. How did it come to this? I think about that day and night, you know. My dreams are full of children. Marlyne and I liked to make love. We suited each other well. We were both modest but ardent. We needed it to be dark. We couldn't feel at ease in the light, each of us judging our own bodies with a severe eye. Since childhood I've suffered from a skin disease. I'm terribly ashamed of it, even though it's not my fault. I see myself as uglier than I am, obviously, since Marlyne desired me, loved me. She caressed me with no disgust. Yes, Marlyne is the only woman with whom I've had what they call complete sexual relations. I was afraid of my body, the look of it—my red, dry, scaly skin. But no. Nothing so terrible in the end. Marlyne caressed me, she wanted to rub up against that coarse, scratchy skin, have that poor suffering skin against her own, she liked it, her orgasms were never faked. Or maybe they were? I don't know. No, I don't think so. That's not how it seems to me. We had a good sex life, easy, sweet. Nothing complicated. Sometimes Marlyne was thin, sometimes she was round, I'm not sure anymore. It didn't matter to me. How can I put this? I was making love with her, with her personality as Marlyne, with my wife. I couldn't describe her body for you. What does it matter? All my wife's bodies suited me. Is that wrong of me? Is it to my credit? Ah, but I couldn't care less. I can't describe my own body. I don't like it, it changes, I don't want to know anything about it. I liked my wife's body however it was because it was her body, my wife's, and because I liked to make love with Marlyne, with that particular woman whose name is Marlyne and whose belly had housed my children. I didn't ask that body of Marlyne's to please me any more than my own pleased me. I didn't look at it, it didn't interest me. But when we took each other in our arms, each of us having taken off our pajamas, both naked beneath the comforter pulled up to our chins, then we were happy, so what could our shapes or appearances matter? We were happy because we were so at home with each other. How did it come to this? Marlyne was a peerless mother, you know!"

Gilles Principaux pulled a handkerchief from his pocket, wiped his eyes.

Mᵉ Susane had the impression the chair was just barely holding back Gilles's body, crumbled and liquefied by despair.

She kept a close eye on him, ready to spring forward and stop him from falling off.

She found herself moved beyond what she thought it acceptable and decent to feel about Principaux.

Which is why, bitter, almost vindictive, after a long silence that would have seemed abnormal and therefore uncomfortable to anyone who thought themselves sane but which did not seem to bother Principaux, she asked, in a low, muffled voice:

"Monsieur Principaux, have we met before?"

He didn't understand, or pretended not to.

He frowned, already almost bored, then raised his eyebrows, politely feigning interest.

"Monsieur Principaux, did we meet when I was a child?

When I was maybe ten years old, and you fourteen or fifteen? Do you, if that encounter ever took place, remember me?"

Me Susane laid her trembling hands, unashamed, on the table.

She calmly clasped one with the other, making no attempt to hide that she was trying to keep them still.

"Do you remember me?" she said again.

"I have no idea," said Principaux.

Then, annoyed:

"But really, what does it matter . . ."

"It matters a great deal," said Me Susane, "and please don't take that tone."

He gave her an unsettled smile, though Me Susane couldn't determine whether he was sincerely troubled by the strangeness of the situation, or if he found this Me Susane alarming for reasons that had nothing to do with him, or if, perhaps, in the dark gleam of Me Susane's eyes, he recognized something—but what, what look of delight or terror, beaming or frightened, what did he see? she wondered.

"I don't understand you, I don't know what you're talking about," said Principaux wearily. "What matters here is Marlyne, it's my wife. Why should I remember you? I really don't understand."

"Try anyway, push yourself!"

Feeling like a hopeless coward, Me Susane gave a little laugh to lessen, to dilute, to undo the intense seriousness of her words.

He relaxed ever so slightly.

"But why do you insist I make that effort? Whether we've met before or not, what could it matter?"

"Then why did you choose me as your wife's lawyer?"

"I don't know . . . A matter of chance . . . We needed some-one, didn't we? It could have been anyone, I came across your name, and that was that."

He heaved a bored sigh, spread his arms slightly to under-score the inanity of this conversation.

"You're not doing much to establish a trusting relationship," he said acerbically. "You're kind of strange."

"I turned strange when I was ten years old."

Mᵉ Susane gave him a big smile, leaning back in her chair.

After some hesitation, Principaux answered with a smile that valiantly, perhaps good-heartedly, strove to measure up to hers.

What was there in the heart of Principaux's heart?

Who, to her, was this anxious-eyed, ordinary-faced man?

The violent impression she'd felt when Principaux first walked into her office, the sense that she'd met him long be-fore in Caudéran, and that that one encounter, that curious battle, had brought about "Maître Susane," that impression she no longer felt.

He was simply there before her, a body dead to her memory.

Why did she still place such faith in that first, fleeting, patchy impression, why did she feel she had to cling to it as to a declaration of loyalty toward the little girl she was back then, even if that little girl, that little Susane girl, had not been mistreated in Principaux's bedroom?

Since the boy, she was almost certain, had done her no harm, nothing she hadn't consented to, perhaps even aspired to.

What would she have become without that?

Nothing much, nothing much . . .

Nonetheless, she felt a sort of hatred—toward all the Principauxs, toward everyone in that family.

She roused herself, forced herself to offer him a coffee, which he accepted, she thought, with relief, as if convinced he'd come through a difficult moment unscathed.

He broke into a smile when her eyes turned his way.

That was how the reporters had filmed him: cheerful and quietly anxious, smiling too brightly but at the same time on the defensive.

No matter how he behaved, it wasn't right.

He seemed to Me Susane at once naïve and guileful, sly and openhearted.

She found that unnerving.

Because she didn't understand it.

She was setting Principaux's coffee cup down on the desk when the telephone rang, the landline she almost never used.

She recognized the voice of her mother, Madame Susane, distant, as if muffled by sadness and regret, a secret voice, faraway:

"It's me, darling, I'm calling you at your office, forgive me, but I can't get hold of you on your cell phone, I'm not disturbing you too much?"

"No."

"Listen . . . I remember now . . . Can you hear me?"

"Yes, yes."

"Oh, good. Those people in Caudéran whose house I took you to when you were little, I remember their name, it came to me all of a sudden . . ."

"Yes?"

Me Susane, shaken, took the receiver away from her ear.

Principaux was blowing on his coffee to cool it down, like a child.

"Are you there, darling? Do you hear me?"

"Yes!"

"Their name was Majuraux, like the wine, you know, but not spelled quite the same. Not Principaux, Majuraux. I remember now."

"Are you sure?" said Me Susane breathlessly. "Really sure?"

Her mother stayed silent for so long that Me Susane, alarmed, tried to bring her back:

"Mama, are you there?"

"Yes."

"You're sure of what you're telling me? Really sure?"

"No, but . . . almost. I'd say, maybe, sixty percent."

"I see."

"To be honest, darling, to be conservative . . . I might make it twenty-five percent sure that was those people's name, Majuraux, *a-u-x,* no *e.*"

"Really, Mama!"

Me Susane gave Principaux, who had looked up from his cup with a slightly questioning air, a wide, reassuring smile.

He returned it, mechanically: vast rows of teeth, prominent cheekbones, trembling eyes.

"Mama," sighed Me Susane, "what's the point of telling me this if you're so unsure of it? You get me all worked up, and then what you tell me is so shaky I can't do anything with it, you understand?"

"Yes, darling, I'm sorry, I have to hang up now, your father's coming. Don't forget: Majuraux, *a-u-x*. There's the Majureaux vineyard, with an *e,* but it's not the same thing, they're two different families. Now that I've given it some thought, I really am quite convinced it was the Majuraux house we went to. I don't believe I've ever met a Principaux, although how to be sure, right, after so long? Majuraux, though, yes, I think so, darling. No guarantees, mind you! I have to go now, your father's coming, you know how all this exasperates him. It literally drives him crazy, yes . . . Adieu, darling, adieu . . ."

On January 30, a Wednesday morning, through Me Susane's intercession, Rudy and little Lila made Sharon's acquaintance in Me Susane's apartment, where it was more or less agreed that Sharon would look after Lila until evening.

Rudy had suggested a flat fee that Me Susane then passed on to Sharon.

Without admitting it to Rudy, though, she'd raised the price, not that she found the sum on offer too low (in which case she would have told him so outright, would even have sternly expressed her disapproval), but because she had a deep, fervent, inexpressible desire to see Lila looked after by a happy Sharon, pleased with her lot, even secretly delighted at the windfall.

From Lila's birth, Me Susane had felt a gentle, melancholy, sunny love for the child.

She wouldn't have wanted to be Lila's mother, or anyone else's.

It suited her very well not to be, on this earth, anyone's mother.

That another woman had given birth to the exquisite Lila and that she, Me Susane, labored discreetly, serenely for her goddaughter-in-spirit's happiness, that suited her perfectly.

She knew her unbreakable affection for Rudy had influenced and even created her fondness for Lila, that she wanted to love and protect Lila because she cared about Rudy's happiness, even if she sometimes denied it.

It had always seemed to her that should Rudy slip into sorrow, despair, and then ruination her own disaster would come with it, even if there was no logical reason why one should lead to the other, save that they both came from the same world.

It mattered to her, oh, how it mattered, that Rudy be quietly, nicely prosperous, that he flourish and grow in wealth and felicity: they were, him and Me Susane, two communicating vessels, and were Rudy to fail in his work as in his life as a man, Me Susane believed she would suffer that failure's inevitable repercussions, that the churning waters he was struggling in would wash into her life, filling it with a mud she would never be free of.

They were, it seemed to her, bound together like accomplices in a larceny—that of having extracted themselves, discreet, wary, ambitious, and self-contained, from a background that they in no way sought to take pride in, not that they renounced it or felt any shame at it.

Neither would make themselves the spokesperson for their family.

They were alone, reserved, even secretive with their colleagues about their proletarian origins—but secretive in a neutral, cold way, with no sign (they were both sure) of even the shadow of a sense of inferiority.

But if Rudy ran off course . . .

It was important to Me Susane to see in Lila a manifestation of Rudy's success, of his entrance into something beautiful, serious, and old, from which he would never be expelled.

Because Lila's mother came from an old Saint-Émilion family.

And so, without having set out to do so, Rudy was implanting himself.

He'd appealed, he'd seduced, he'd conceived.

His child's grandparents were people who once gave orders to his own father.

He'd pulled himself up solely through the power of his thoughtfulness, his chivalrous virility, his fruitful seed.

And the fact that, by chance and by luck, Lila looked like Rudy confirmed Me Susane in her affection for that little girl.

Her own parents, Monsieur and Madame Susane, had fallen ludicrously in love with Lila.

They loved her, yes, as their daughter's daughter, and they fell into a cross, contentious, skeptical silence whenever Me Susane found herself having to remind them that Lila had a mother who wasn't her, Me Susane, and that that mother, for all (according to Rudy) her shortcomings, still had full rights over Lila's upbringing, she could love Lila and look after her in a way the Susanes disapproved of, and that was none of their business, they who would never be anything other than backup grandparents.

Because yes, from the start, only with the greatest difficulty did Monsieur and Madame Susane consent to acknowledge that obvious truth, that simple state of affairs, only with a stubborn, sulking chagrin that discouraged Me Susane from trying to make them see reason.

Such that, when she allowed herself to remember it, she had to confess that she'd sometimes given up trying to disabuse them, given up fighting their fierce, dark, mute belief that she was Lila's one, proper, true mother.

And even Lila's biological mother, they very nearly thought, Me Susane was convinced.

Had they not, on that subject, made a number of supposedly playful allusions, stamped with a cynical humor that wasn't in their nature?

Had they not, on learning of Lila's birth (how, Me Susane couldn't remember—directly from Rudy, from her, from the birth announcements in *Sud Ouest*?), cried out to her:

"You come and see us so rarely, you could have been pregnant and given birth without our ever knowing! You tell us Rudy's involved with another woman, that's news to us! We've never seen this other woman! This supposed solicitor's clerk!"

They joked with a sort of indignant fury and as if shocked as much as outraged at having to banter about such a thing.

Why was Lila not simply the daughter of their only daughter

and Rudy, whom they considered their son-in-law? Why did everything have to be twisted, frustrating, unnameable?

Stung by such unfairness, Me Susane had stammered:

"B-but I visit you all the time, why do you say you rarely see me..."

"You show up and you're gone, we can't even remember you've been here. So what you consider 'all the time' becomes 'almost never' in our memory. Oh, I'm quite sure," Madame Susane added loftily, "I'm quite sure you can show us your appointment book with 'visit parents' checked ten times a month, that won't change a thing about what we feel, and isn't that what matters?"

It seemed that Monsieur and Madame Susane had gone from an embittered impression that Me Susane was neglecting them to an equally painful but considerably more far-fetched conviction that she'd clandestinely given birth to Rudy's daughter and, for reasons that would always elude their grasp, their understanding, their forgiveness, was lying to them about it.

Nothing would ever convince them to give up on that fantastical certainty, Me Susane told herself.

Not even the results of a DNA test, which she would never dream of showing them, refusing to follow them into their madness, not even a DNA test would do anything to pull them out of it—out of that madness, that faith, that cruel hope.

That's why they so love to watch over Lila, Me Susane did not say to Rudy.

They're very fond of you, yes, but if they're always happy to look after Lila it's because they think they're her biological grandparents, she would have told Rudy had she dared.

But, she sometimes wondered with a certain terror, could they not have got hold of DNA evidence, obsessed as they were, behind her back?

She thought them entirely capable of sending a sample of Lila's saliva and a few of Me Susane's hairs to some American laboratory and saying nothing about it, just as they would say nothing about concealing a putative positive test result, they were, yes, mad enough to find a sour delight in knowing they were Lila's grandparents beyond all possible doubt, and keeping what they knew from Me Susane!

Beyond all possible doubt, they would think, in their na-ïveté, their ignorance, and their senselessness!

Any test showing a genetic bond between Me Susane and Lila would of course be in error, thought Me Susane, unable to repress an exasperated chuckle, but her unschooled parents would never suspect such a thing!

She'd often held back from saying to them straight out: If you've had a DNA test done and you were told I'm Lila's mother, you must understand that the test was wrong, you must realize that those tests aren't a hundred percent reliable and as a matter of fact there are lots of scams in that business.

She might have added, with a little laugh whose cutting, furious edge would have escaped them: The best test is me telling you no, I am not Lila's mother.

But she hadn't, not wanting to cast anchor in the depths of their delusions.

Because they would innocently come up with ways to keep her prisoner there, with oblique assertions and twisting, turning questions, sniffing untrustingly, raising their eyebrows, until Me Susane found herself, first worn down and then caught up in their spell, perfectly at home in her parents' delirium.

Sometimes she wondered if she wasn't *caught up already*.

When, that Wednesday morning, she opened her door to Rudy and Lila, went through the introductions with a particularly gracious and engaging Sharon, then delivered Lila of her many layers of winter clothes, down to the girl's plump little body in T-shirt and tights, she told herself, pressing that heavy, dense, little-child flesh to her breast: I love this girl as if she were my own.

It was very warm at Me Susane's.

She'd turned up the thermostat, wanting everything to be just right for Lila.

Now Me Susane was sweltering in her own apartment.

She noticed that Rudy was too hot as well, and also that he was in a hurry to go off to work.

He stood fidgeting by the front door, eager to be gone, as Me Susane peppered Sharon with instructions.

"Sharon, when you go out for a walk with Lila, don't forget to put her scarf on her, and remember, Sharon, that Lila mustn't eat dried fruit, apparently, Sharon, dried fruit can kill her, and also, according to her father, it would be good for Lila to take a nap, thanks, Sharon, for agreeing to look after Lila, thanks so much, really."

Oddly encouraged by Rudy's presence, by his broad shoulders and his punctilious levelheadedness and as if she needed a witness at long last, she added, falsely casual:

"And, Sharon, how about that marriage certificate? Have you managed to come up with it?"

"I've already explained about that, Madame Susane."

"H—" Me Susane interrupted, citing her first name, which Sharon still balked at using, no matter how many times Me Susane had told her she couldn't feel right calling her Sharon unless Sharon agreed to call her by her first name.

Sharon still never had.

She found ways to avoid it, and then sometimes, needlessly, threw out a "Madame Susane" that hurt Me Susane as much as it irritated her.

Sharon, speaking my name will not put you in any danger, it won't meld you with the villainy you believe I'm marked with. What do you smell on me, Sharon, that so fills you with disgust at the thought of me getting close to you, physically as well as spiritually? What do you believe is the nature, Sharon, of the smell I give off? You know things about me I don't know myself!

"I don't remember you telling me anything specific about it," she said cunningly.

"Yes, I did, have you forgotten?"

Sharon, surprised, smiling, tried with a tactful, sidelong glance to enlist Rudy as an ally, but he was looking at his phone, and to Me Susane's great relief wasn't listening.

"Yes, yes," Sharon went on, not looking at Me Susane, "I told you last time, my marriage certificate is held up back in Mauritius."

"What do you mean by 'held up'?" Me Susane said in a very soft, cautious voice.

"Well, held up. I explained that last time."

"But, Sharon, when was that?"

"I don't know, last time, you can't expect me to remember the date. I told you, there are people back in Mauritius who are hanging on to my marriage certificate."

"H-hanging on to it?"

Me Susane was stammering like a backward child, mumbling and lost, afraid.

With what looked like commiseration, Sharon raised her soft lips toward Me Susane's ear.

"I told you, certain people I've asked to send that paper have no intention of doing so, simply because I need it. Those people are hoping we'll have to come home, they want us to fail, yes, there are such people, you know. For the moment there's nothing I can do, you're not going to get my marriage certificate, there's really nothing I can do," added Sharon in a voice far sorrier for Me Susane than for herself.

And with that she bent down toward Lila, as if Me Susane had been keeping her, with these pointless questions, from a mission of far greater importance.

She knelt before Lila, put her hands under the T-shirt, and caressed the child's back.

Lila groaned in pleasure.

She rubbed her fat cheeks against Sharon's forehead.

"Mmm, mmm, little rabbit, your fur is soft, little rabbit," Sharon was whispering.

Slight, delicate, she seemed, thought Me Susane, to make herself even smaller next to Lila, as if curling up inside herself so as not to frighten the child by her grown-up dimensions.

"Looks like a connection's been made," whispered Rudy, giving Me Susane a sweet, happy-father smile.

She then felt (just for a moment!) as if she'd been thought of or acknowledged as Lila's mother, as the mother of that imperfect, heavenly, loyal little girl.

At day's end, after many hours spent trying to clear up Sharon's situation, Sharon who, she realized with a secret, derisive little laugh, would never do anything to help her, Me Susane came home in a dark and peevish mood, even vaguely resolving to tell Sharon she wouldn't go on working for her or her family if she kept up this ridiculous insistence on hampering the file's progress, and found Lila and Sharon sharing a cozy, cheerful dinner in the blinding gleam of the lights, every one of which was turned on.

She saw at once that Sharon had whipped up a child-size love feast.

And, grateful, slightly concerned, she admired Sharon's astute professional sensibility, for having evidently inspired Lila to idolize her in such short order.

The little girl cried out something that Me Susane interpreted as: It's delicious, what a wonderful meal! Or: I love Sharon! Or possibly: I want to stay with Sharon for my whole life!

The sharp point of a brand-new pain pierced Me Susane's heart.

Her parents, who loved Lila with a primitive, immutable, faithful love, had never, when she stayed with them, thought of making her a meal like the one Sharon set before her that evening.

Monsieur and Madame Susane, indifferent to food, presented Lila with frozen dishes they'd bought on sale and preserved in outlandish, extravagant quantities in their big basement freezer, explaining that they couldn't at the same time do the shopping and remember what they'd already stored away, so they built up absurd stockpiles of food and then, after five or ten years, tossed out what they hadn't eaten, just as blithely as they'd bought it.

They were delighted that Lila was not a fussy eater, considering it an added moral strength of their beloved Lila that she voiced no complaint as she downed the adulterated slop that, easily satisfied, all capacity for judgment denatured, they'd made their daily fare.

Me Susane had tried to warn them off that:

"Lila's too fat, she needs a carefully considered diet."

They objected:

"We eat the same thing, and we're not too fat. It's nothing to do with us."

Me Susane wasn't sure that her parents had not grown much too fat.

They'd changed since she was a child, she remembered them as a lean couple, their flesh efficient, economical, concise.

But what does it matter, she said to herself, they're gaining weight as they age and they don't know it, they're happy with themselves and each other, what does it matter that they're making their way together, always united, erotically bound, toward an undeniable corpulence?

"Lila's too young, you have to teach her good habits. The doctor weighed her, she's over the average for a girl her age," she explained to them all the same.

"Oh, doctors!" Monsieur Susane puffed, forcing a disdainful laugh, because lack of respect for the experts wasn't his way.

"Lila's just fine as she is," added Madame Susane, categorically.

Sharon had served Lila fine slices of milk-fed lamb on a bed of grilled zucchini and eggplant.

She'd made a light sauce with fresh mint and almond milk.

Me Susane would later finish the leftovers and find them delicious.

Why could Monsieur and Madame Susane not care for Lila as tenderly and devotedly as Sharon, they who privately insisted that Lila was their biological granddaughter?

Their fierce love for Lila was the love of true grandparents, but their lack of interest in her health seemed to say they knew their connection with her was not so incontestable that they could endure the tedious constraint of coming up with balanced meals.

There Me Susane felt sorry for them.

But what could she do? she asked herself.

Falsely confess that she'd given birth to Lila seven years before?

Or sternly rebuke them for feeding Lila mediocre foods, as they wouldn't do, perhaps, with the flesh of their flesh?

Me Susane hadn't long been home from the office when

Rudy came to pick up Lila, Rudy at first anxious and on edge and then so relieved when the little girl pressed her forehead to his belly and hugged him with all her might that he cried out to Me Susane as to Sharon, in a voice filled with gratitude:

"Thank you, thank you!"

Because Lila didn't usually make a show of her feelings when she was happy, and the child Rudy most often found waiting for him, even at Monsieur and Madame Susane's, where everything always went fine, was a coldly sullen one, happy in her indiscernible way, her grave, closed, silent way.

"I've never seen my Lila so overjoyed," he told Me Susane on the phone the next morning. "Sharon knew just how to be with her, like no one ever has, not her mother or me or your wonderful parents. She even told me she'd eaten the best meal of her life."

Me Susane answered that she was delighted to hear it.

She felt proud, of Sharon and of herself.

Then, after they'd said their customary parting words before hanging up, and as if Rudy had waited for that moment so as to give what he wanted to say a casual spin:

"Oh, I understand Sharon and Lila went out shopping together, then Sharon took her to an apartment where she was supposed to work, you know, to do the cleaning. Apparently Lila didn't mind at all. She explored the whole place, she rode horseback on Sharon's vacuum cleaner, she even helped her turn over a mattress—well, maybe I'm misrepresenting what I think I heard . . ."

"Sharon took Lila to another employer's house? A house we don't know anything about? That's what Lila told you?"

Scandalized, Me Susane did her best to keep her tone neutral, failing to fool Rudy.

"Don't worry, Lila seemed absolutely thrilled!" he hurried to add, perhaps fearing, thought Me Susane, that she might not let Sharon go on looking after Lila over such a trifle. "And anyway, what does it matter?" he asked, not without courage. "You told me yourself, Sharon is serious and trustworthy, irreproachable, right? In that case she can take Lila wherever she likes, as far as I'm concerned."

"Yes, you're right," said Me Susane, a brutal wave of relief leaving her weak all over.

Yes, why not, let Lila be led wherever Sharon chooses—Sharon, that guardian angel—and let Lila enlighten us all!

And so, the evening of that same cold, gloomy day, the first sentence Me Susane spoke to Sharon, wanting, she told herself, to set matters straight, was this:

"Sharon, I hear you went to another employer's with Lila."

She spoke as softly as she could, and just as quiet was her footstep on the floorboards, *so she wouldn't see the pheasant fly off or the little goat bolt out of rifle range.* "But it's not a problem, Sharon, since Lila's father told me this morning he couldn't see anything wrong with it. He's the judge, right?"

Sharon, tiny, her face upturned and attentive, hard and almost creased under the effervescent LEDs, let out a quick laugh of surrender, then lowered her eyes.

"Yes," she said quietly, "I did go to Madame Principaux's, I can't just walk out on her like that."

"I won't say another word about it," Me Susane murmured. "In any case, it's fine with Lila's father. He's the judge, right?"

"That's right."

Now Sharon's voice seemed forceful and proud, provocative.

"The mama didn't say anything against it?"

"The mama?" Me Susane sputtered. "What mama?"

"Lila's mama? She's not against me taking the little one to Madame Principaux's?"

"I have no idea, I suppose not but I really don't know, it's all up to the father. My God, Sharon, it's not my place to question Lila's mother. Lila's mama," she cravenly corrected, to please Sharon.

"You don't know her?" asked Sharon after many long seconds of suspicion and disbelief.

"Lila's mother? The mama?"

Sharon said nothing.

Her blue-green gaze was fixed, inclement, on Me Susane's face far above her.

"Well, no, I know who she is but I've never met her, so what? But I do know who she is, anyway. What do you mean, Sharon, by 'know'? 'Be friends with' or 'be aware of'?"

"Whatever you like," Sharon murmured.

As if suddenly exhausted, she slowly reached out and took her jacket from the coatrack.

She touched her bare neck with one hand and curtly asked:

"Did you see, I put your orange scarf on the little one when the papa came to pick her up."

Me Susane had noticed no such thing the evening before,

she wasn't even sure she'd told Lila goodbye, absorbed as she was in her discussion with Rudy of her client who wanted to change his name.

"You did the right thing, thanks. Sharon . . ."

Me Susane held her breath.

Then, gasping, stumbling over her words, she went on:

"What can I do to take care of this marriage certificate business? And your file? I need that paper, you know."

"Ah," said Sharon, "I have faith in you. Any idea you have will be a good idea, whatever you decide will be the right thing. There's nothing I can do. That's your job, saving people who can't do anything. Every evening my first prayer goes not to God but to Me Susane."

And then, in the hallway, Sharon dropped to her knees, heavily, painfully, even though the weight she carried on this earth was next to nothing.

"I kneel down like this, you see, and I talk to you, and I beg you to come to our aid. Only after that do I talk to God. Because I know everything you do will be the right thing."

Shocked, Me Susane briskly pulled Sharon to her feet.

"That's—that's not good," she stammered, "you mustn't think that way, you mustn't have such high hopes . . ."

Beneath her fingers, she could feel Sharon's frail humerus, the dense, meager flesh of that insignificant woman who now occupied a place in her thoughts as substantial as Marlyne Principaux's.

Sharon, I cannot stand prayers, I cannot abide that maudlin feminine piety, that calculating, scheming hopefulness! Sharon, do not give me a role in the sentimental little drama you put on in your strange and at the same time commonplace thoughts, do not pray, Sharon, to me! It makes me so ashamed!

The next day, when Me Susane set out for the office in that strange winter's hyperborean cold, she wasn't wearing her rubber-soled boots.

Vaguely telling herself it was a mistake, she'd put on a pair of heeled ankle boots.

Maybe Principaux would be paying her a visit?

But wasn't she hoping more to intimidate Principaux than to charm him?

Faced with Principaux's hypothetical presence, she wanted to feel a self-assurance she would find far more in spiky little heels than in rubber soles, even if the bravado that came with the heels, the poise afforded as much by a heightened stature (and Me Susane was already so tall!) as by the absolute, unyielding, tyrannical authority of their click-clack on the sonorous wooden floor, seemed not all that powerful in the face of Principaux and his self-proclaimed lack of memory of their long-ago encounter—the dominion he (perhaps) granted himself over Me Susane's memory.

Sometimes, vaguely, she asked herself:

Suppose Mama isn't wrong? Suppose it was the Majuraux house we went to, not the Principaux house? In that case, what would Gilles Principaux be to me? Nothing at all, apart from Marlyne's husband. Who am I supposed to be before that man?

And so, that morning, she'd chosen to appear to him, should he come to the office, as a woman in spike heels, authoritarian, glamorously despotic in her resounding footfalls.

She wanted not to please him but to daunt him, not to appeal to him but to lessen him, that man with the hollow torso, with his dull blue shirts beneath his crewneck sweaters.

She'd succumbed to vanity, to weakness, she would tell herself once she was back on her feet, and her fear of Principaux had led her into the foolishness of the heels.

Yes, she was afraid of him—furiously, with no sort of certainty, and well aware that he couldn't tell her, as she'd heard him say in a dream:

That was a Majuraux you ran into back then, your mother isn't mistaken, it was only two weeks ago that you met me, Principaux.

Ah, I got what was coming to me, she would think, for being mediocre enough to be afraid of him and to want to command his respect by a simulacrum of power.

She'd been walking with her usual broad strides.

The smooth soles of her delicate ankle boots slipped on the icy paving stones of the Allées de Tourny.

Suddenly she fell.

Her forehead struck the pavement.

She couldn't feel the wound, the blood flowing over her brow, so terrible was the pain in her left knee.

Dreadfully embarrassed, she immediately tried to stand up.

But her knee gave way, she collapsed again.

Her cheek struck the ground, and, as after an unexpected, undeserved slap, a rush of stunned tears came to her eyes.

She was so ashamed, of her failings, of her inadequacies, that she resolutely pushed away the hands that came to her aid.

"I'll be fine, thanks—thanks," she stammered.

At the price of an agony she could have spared herself by accepting the support of those anonymous hands, she stood up on her trembling legs, walked on with tiny little steps.

Blood was dripping from her forehead onto her lips.

Her knee was hurting her horribly.

She limped to the office.

How she wished she could call Madame Susane!

Why, my God, can I not call my mother?

How did the three of us get here, a loving daughter, loving parents, how did this happen that I can't ask them to come and console me, bandage my soul, tend to my wound?

She struggled up the two flights of stairs, clutching the banister an arm's length ahead of her and then hoisting herself so her left foot could touch the steps as lightly as possible.

At her office door, leaning with both shoulders against the wall, hips outthrust, like a hoodlum in an old movie, Principaux was waiting for her, somber-faced.

Me Susane managed to stifle a little cry of surprise and frustration.

With one hand, she quickly wiped her dirty cheeks.

Principaux gave her a broad, boyish smile.

So friendly was the look on his face that it moved Me Susane in spite of herself.

He didn't seem to notice Me Susane's pronounced limp, or the blood on her forehead.

He was looking at her but not seeing her, which relieved and troubled her at the same time.

"Oh, there you are!" he cried, like a delighted child.

He looked Me Susane over, from her face to her feet—not even a child but a young dog, a happy animal, she told herself, slightly uncomfortable.

"Can you see me now? Do you have a little time? Should I have made an appointment?" he was now asking, his voice pleading, almost whining.

Can't you see I'm injured? Bleeding?

But that Me Susane didn't dare say to him.

Weary but welcoming, she quietly answered:

"No, no, don't give it a thought, you did the right thing, as a matter of fact I was wanting to . . ."

Her voice trailed off to a mumble.

She showed Principaux into the office, then staggered toward the bathroom.

The reflection of her face in the tiny mirror horrified her.

Blood was drying on her eyebrows, on the wings of her nose, was still seeping from the split in her forehead.

She cleaned herself up as best she could.

She combed her hair, put on some lipstick that, she told herself, was too bright a red for the circumstances, hoping she might thereby give herself a presence that her resonant ankle boots couldn't bring her now.

Because it mattered to her, as she faced Principaux, not to be herself.

It mattered to her, as she faced Principaux, to be a woman who cannot be beaten.

He'd already settled in, already taken off his scarf and coat, which he'd neatly folded and set down near his armchair, facing Me Susane's desk.

A violent pain shot through her knee when she sat down.

She gave herself permission to grimace, since Principaux seemed not to be noticing.

And yet he was staring at her face, her painted lips no doubt contorted by pain, and surprise at that pain.

Suddenly his expression turned very serious.

But what he was studying with his aggrieved, wary eye had nothing to do with Me Susane's injured face, which, she realized, he literally did not see.

Anxious and untrusting, he was probing the depths of his own inner disarray.

"Maître, I don't know what to think anymore, I'm very unhappy, I mean even unhappier than last time."

She raised her eyebrows, a lacerating pain shooting through her right temple.

Her head suddenly feeling too heavy, she let it droop over her desk, one hand wedged under her cheek as a prop.

How she was hurting!

"Maître," said Principaux, "I can't understand why Marlyne doesn't want to see me anymore. I went yesterday, she wouldn't come to the visiting room. Maître, help me!"

He began to sob.

"She refused to come to the visiting room, I can't understand why, I only say nice things to her, words of love, I never ask questions, she can hardly be afraid of me, can she? I'm gentle, I'm understanding, can't you see? I'm a gentle, understanding victim!"

Bewilderment, sorrow, and concern raised Principaux's voice to a pitch painful to Me Susane's ear.

Could the young Principaux, in his Caudéran bedroom, have had such a strident voice? Wouldn't she have remembered that?

How she was hurting!

She thought she felt blood trickling from her wound, again soiling her cheeks, and her blood-clogged eyelashes preventing the lid from moistening her pupils, which was why her eyes were so dry, as if someone had thrown a handful of ash in her face!

She forced herself not to put her hands to her cheeks, not to apologize for her appearance.

Since in any case Principaux didn't see her.

"I'm the victim here, aren't I, Maître? Me and the children?"

Now Principaux was weeping quietly.

"Leave her alone," Mᵉ Susane choked out. "Don't torment yourself. She doesn't want to see you, let it go. What can it matter to you? Why do you insist on seeing her? To convince yourself that you love her? She's tortured by your presence, you're tormented by hers, don't go back."

Had she really spoken those words?

Dazed by pain, Mᵉ Susane wasn't sure she had, particularly because Principaux was still looking at her expectantly, as if waiting for her to make up her mind to answer him.

He'd reached into his pocket and taken out a large handkerchief, clean and tidily pressed, which he slowly, carefully unfolded before dabbing at his eyes.

"Tell me," said Mᵉ Susane, "about when you got home and found the police and Marlyne in the living room . . ."

Just as she'd foreseen, Principaux was roused by those words.

His hands began to tremble, so violently that he had to resign himself to crumpling his handkerchief before putting it back in his pocket, incapable of folding it.

A fixed, incongruous smile turned up the corners of his lips, the same misplaced smile that Me Susane had seen on his face in his interviews, on which she refused to pass judgment, unlike certain commentators, who saw it as a sign of Principaux's depravity.

All at once she thought it obvious that this rictus allowed Principaux to conceal his rage, his profound sense of being misunderstood.

It was, she suddenly saw, an unfortunate reflex of his natural reserve, a clumsy display of his notion of propriety, which dictated that neither sorrow nor anger must ever be shown.

"Because yes, Maître," he began, emotion garbling half his words, "as you know Marlyne called me earlier, I was on campus, I was working, and she called to ask me to come home, to order me to come home actually, which, it's true, annoyed me. Because I had a lot to do that day. Because yes, Maître, I could say I was swamped that day. Because yes, I still had a number of administrative tasks to deal with, I had to see students, fill out spreadsheets, write up reports, not to mention a long string of emails that had been weighing on my mind since that morning when I opened my inbox and saw that a minor little problem I'd pointed out to my colleagues and the administration had brought me a flood of responses and reactions I would gladly have done without, and I thought to myself, I mean I thought, that I would have been smarter not to say anything, not to bring up a little problem that at the time, it's true, I didn't consider so little but not so important either that it should bring me this wave of answers. Because, Maître, I could have felt flattered at that, right? Right?"

Mᵉ Susane didn't answer.

She thought she felt blood on her face.

Her knee was throbbing so cruelly that the mere thought of having to stand up sent her into a panic.

"Because, Maître, yes, some of my colleagues would have made much of that, boasted about it, turned it to their advantage," Principaux went on, tripping heatedly over his words, "because, yes, you mention something almost in passing, something you care about, having to do with religion, or secularism, in this case it's the same, and then, and then one thing leads to another and grows and expands till it all starts to get a bit overwhelming and you could reap glittering rewards from that if you're ambitious, which, Maître, I'm not, probably not enough, and from all that back-and-forth I reaped only ashes that will never, Maître, bring me glory or fortune. Because yes, I'm a nice man, a gentle, peaceful man, I'm a naïve man, yes, Maître. Because I am a credulous man, Maître. Because I am, Maître, a—"

She cut him off:

"What happened when you got home?"

Now it felt as if the blood from her wound was dripping off her chin onto the collar of her blouse.

What was he seeing?

She didn't dare make a move.

Now her hands were resting, ponderous and enormous, between her equally heavy, petrified thighs.

"Oh yes, Maître, when I got home on that fateful day!"

He tried to feign a laugh, then stopped short.

But he was still smiling, distracted, oblivious, as his hard, pained gaze lingered on Mᵉ Susane's ear.

"Because yes, Maître, I was in the middle of work when Marlyne called me, she never called me, never disturbed me, and I know you're thinking I should have realized something was terribly wrong. Because no, Maître, I didn't realize that, and I should have. Maître, I will never forgive myself for that, even if I know it wouldn't have changed anything and Marlyne performed her act immediately after she'd called me, or almost. Because I would have rushed home, and then what? Yes, Maître, and then what? Because I would have found the children before the police got there. Because I would have found the children dead anyway. Because, Maître, technically that wouldn't have changed anything, would it? Because I was irritated by her call? Yes, I was impatient, unhappy, she didn't have anything to tell me, she whispered: 'Can you come home, please? Oh, if you could come home right away,' and when I asked her why, telling her that just then I had loads to do, far too much for my liking, she only repeated in a moaning, piteous voice, annoying, yes, not exactly the kind of voice that makes you want to obey: 'Come home, please come home.' Because I should have realized? Because no one would have realized, Maître. Because I had a thousand things to do that day. Because nevertheless I went home much earlier than I'd planned, Maître, no one ever mentions that. Because I resigned myself, because a dull little worry began to nag at me, Maître. I went home before the usual time. Because little by little irritation was being replaced by terror, because time, even a short time, makes us rethink our first reactions, yes, Maître. Because an hour after Marlyne's call I wasn't put out anymore, because I was tormented, yes. Because I drove faster than usual. Because I was preoccupied, yes, because all of a sudden I was afraid for my wife, for Marlyne, because I told myself maybe something's really wrong with her, why did she call when she never does that, maybe she's depressed, even though, Maître, I couldn't think why Marlyne might be depressed, because from what I could see, Maître, she was fine, she was just fine, because she was still herself the morning of that awful day and the day before too, because she was herself all the time, yes, Maître, because Marlyne's mood never changed, because she was stable and very peaceful, Maître, because Marlyne was, Maître, yes, a well-balanced woman, Maître, a steady woman whom I loved absolutely and whom, Maître, yes, I understood, whom I loved, because a reasonable woman, because a reasonable woman whom, Maître, I loved and, yes, understood completely."

Out of breath, Principaux stopped.

He wasn't smiling anymore, but he was still grimacing so intensely that it deformed his entire face.

He closed his eyes.

Me Susane seized the opportunity (*why, since he wasn't seeing her?*) to put her heavy, reticent hand to her brow, and she thought her wound was still oozing but the blood wasn't flowing with the horrifying abundance she could clearly, indisputably feel before.

"Because yes, Maître, I got home, because there I was and I saw the police were there, parked in front of our quiet house, our quiet life, because then I realized, Maître, that something serious had happened, that something bad had happened to Marlyne, because she was still and will always be my beloved wife, the only woman I will ever love until the day I die, because she's Marlyne and the woman I love and the mother of my children for all time, no matter what, the only children who will be born of me in this world, because, Maître, yes, because yes I got home and my life changed course forever because I will never have another child with anyone because I could of course procreate again because I don't want to because the mere thought of it fills me with horror because I don't want another child, never, I stopped in front of our beloved house, my beloved wife, because then I spotted the police car and I thought Oh no, my love, oh no, I don't want you to be dead because I was only thinking of Marlyne because I'd never really worried about the children who thanks to Marlyne enjoyed magnificent health, because I got home, because I went inside and I found my beloved Marlyne sitting on the couch because the police had sat her down there because Marlyne was an obedient woman because to a fault because sometimes I told her she should stand up for herself at work and not let herself be mistreated by a tyrant of a middle school principal because that's what I might call that man in Pauillac she claimed she respected and admired but who forced her to take on a number of overtime hours that could only damage her mental health because my beloved wife, my love, was what they call a fragile personality, because she was fragile because she was fragile and sensitive because her own mother and sisters because they'd abandoned her because you know that because they almost never came to see her once our children were born

and as if, my God, when she became a mother Marlyne had ir-
reparably fallen because every ideal was turned upside down
like in some dystopian movie where your family criticizes
you rejects you because of your virtue and not your wickedness, because then yes, Maître, her own mother had more or
less resolved to have nothing more to do with Marlyne on the
grounds that Marlyne wasn't living by the respectable but questionable precepts Madame her mother had forged for herself
about a wife's duty to be economically independent, because
I have no objection to that because if my poor little Julia had
lived I would have taught her the same thing because I'm not
the man people think I am or Marlyne's mother thinks I am
because I am a man because I am a father I was a father who
always believed in those ideas of liberation and equality and
Madame her mother thought it better to walk out on Marlyne
than to hear her daughter's firm voice explain that she'd chosen
to be a full-time mother for our children, because Madame her
mother, yes, Maître, opted to desert her plain and simple, to
coldly, cruelly, unforgivably wash her hands of an adult daughter who dared go against her dictates, because, Maître, because I know it because Marlyne suffered terribly because she
suffered from the distance suffered terribly from the distance
brutally imposed by her mother and sisters between themselves and Marlyne, because yes, Maître, those three women
were criminally heartless, because I will never ever forgive
them, because they dumped my dear Marlyne who, no matter
what anyone thinks, always did the best she could, because she
killed because she thought she was doing the best thing she
could, because she believed, it's shocking yes, Maître, but it's

the truth, because it's the truth because she believed she was doing the right thing as she always had before, because she put them to death because she'd always given them everything she could give them and it turns out that death was the best thing she could give them because death was what she thought she had to give them because my poor wife is deranged, Maître, that's obvious, because she's deranged in her quiet and admirable and modest and meritorious way because she deserves our full and complete respect because with my love and support I'm trying to compensate for Madame her mother who doesn't want to hear another word about Marlyne, because it's cruel because it's unspeakable when you're a mother, yes, Maître, because I don't know if you are, because I don't know . . ."

"More or less," murmured Me Susane, exhausted as she'd rarely been before.

"You mean, Maître, that you more or less have children?" Principaux repeated with a sudden amusement that brought back his little-boy smile.

"That's exactly right," said Me Susane curtly. "There's nothing to joke about."

Gripped by a sudden urge to urinate, she struggled to her feet.

She lurched to the bathroom, where she avoided looking at herself in the mirror, sure she would see a poor, blood-smeared face, knowing too that the rational woman in her would doubt the reality of that sight, and she wasn't feeling strong enough to choose between the rational woman and the woman who wasn't but often understood things more rightly.

Who was Principaux to her?

"Because, yes, Maître," he resumed as soon as she was back, "because I came home, because I had to end up coming home, because I had to end up walking inside and seeing, if I may say so! Because what there was to see, I had to see it, didn't I! Because I would have come home anyway, because I would have seen anyway what I had to see, right, Maître? Because seeing what you're shown, because if you're not lucky enough to be blind, because it's inevitable, isn't it, Maître? Because how lucky it would be to be blind in such circumstances, Maître! Because I never asked to see them! Because they made me, Maître! Because I didn't want to see anything, know anything, because I didn't want to look or learn but I only loved Marlyne, Maître. Because I loved my wife more than anything, Maître."

"Who made you, Monsieur Principaux? And made you do what?"

"Gilles, Maître, call me Gilles, Maître, because my name is Gilles."

"I would rather, Monsieur Principaux, not call you Gilles," Me Susane murmured.

In a firmer voice she added:

"I prefer not to call you Gilles. And similarly I'd like you not to call me by my first name."

"I don't even know what it is, now that you mention it," Principaux observed, in a tone of slight surprise.

"Don't know or don't remember?"

She let out a hard little laugh that she immediately regretted, that she was ashamed of.

The pain in her knee sharpened.

"Excuse me," she said calmly.

She leaned to one side, tried to massage the joint, but succeeded only in making it worse.

And her blood-spattered face, how embarrassing!

Never, with Rudy or with any of the few other men whose memory allowed her to vaguely feel that she'd had some sort of sex life, never had she felt her flesh so laid bare.

"Those two guys made me, Maître, the two cops who were there when I got home."

She interrupted:

"Wasn't it a man and a woman? Her young, him close to retirement?"

"No, Maître, not at all, it was two men," said Principaux in the serenely peremptory tone of one who knows his testimony cannot be questioned. "Because two men, no woman, no no, you can be sure I'd remember that, because two fairly old cops, because one string bean and one with a potbelly because they leapt on me the moment I opened the door, because they didn't even let me talk to Marlyne, because they pushed me toward the bedroom because I had no idea what to expect because why force me because, don't you agree, our bedroom should have become a sanctuary the moment Marlyne performed her act because she'd done it, yes, Maître, she'd done it and what had been done was an absolute, don't you agree, Maître, because no one could ever dream or think of undoing it or moderating it or softening its effects, and so, Maître, they pushed me yes pushed me toward that sacred bedroom where my children, Maître, where my children . . ."

Me Susane banished the thought of asking if he'd seen the bodies on the bed or in the bed, exposed or tucked in.

He wiped his pale, gaunt face, his damp eyes.

Me Susane than dared to dab at hers.

How she was hurting, in every way!

Both of them jumped, like accomplices, thought Me Susane, when the desk phone rang.

"It's me, darling..."

Her mother's voice sounded so faint that Me Susane was alarmed:

"Yes, Mama, what's going on? Are you OK?"

"Oh yes. Your father isn't home yet, so I'm taking the opportunity..."

Madame Susane fell silent long enough for Me Susane to start worrying again.

"Hello, Mama? Are you there? Everything OK?"

"Oh yes, darling, don't worry. I wanted to tell you, I was wrong, I was getting things mixed up, in a way. Then I did a funny thing... I ordered my memory to tell me the truth, you see? And it worked."

"Meaning?"

Not wanting to be overheard, Me Susane fell into a low tone, veiled, as if indifferent.

Principaux looked on, eyes still glistening, handkerchief squeezed in his fist.

Did he see Me Susane's pitiful face, her soiled cheeks, the general desolation of her appearance?

"Well, now I know," Madame Susane went on, so muted that Me Susane could scarcely hear her, "I know that that marvelous family was named Ravalet, yes, the Ravalets of Caudéran, darling, if that might help you."

"Mama, Ravalet, really?"

"Yes, now I know, as I was saying, I sort of gave my memory an ultimatum, I commanded it to be precise."

"An ultimatum, but, Mama, your memory had nothing to lose! What was the threat? When you demand something, when you give a command, the other side has to have some consequence to fear! Tell me, what was your memory afraid of?"

Any hope of discretion was swept away by a wave of unexpected anger.

"Mama, you're killing me," she groaned, her lips pressed to the mouthpiece. "You tell me about these supposed Ravalets, but that name has nothing to do with . . . I mean it doesn't even sound anything like Majuraux! Are you sure, are you absolutely sure?"

"Yes, darling, and you're the one who's killing me with your doubts, your skepticism, your cruelty, I don't recognize you. Why don't . . ."

"Mama, I can't hear you, speak louder!"

"Why," Madame Susane resumed, her voice hollow, "why do I feel like you'd only believe me, like you'd only ever love me again if I agreed that their name was Principaux? And once I had I could confess I was lying and you wouldn't even notice, that's the only name you'll accept, and I've never heard of it. Your mind is made up, but you're wrong, darling, you're wrong . . . You're tortured and you're nowhere near the truth, you're suffering for nothing . . . I'm suffering too . . . Ravalet, Ravalet, it was so hard for me to remember that name . . . You're suffering the way you do in a dream, it's real to you but it doesn't exist, darling... Your father's coming, adieu, adieu..."

"Because try to convince Marlyne, I'm begging you!" Principaux burst out an instant after she'd hung up. "Because tell her she has to accept my visits, tell her I can't live without them, the visits I mean, because Marlyne owes me at least that, because who are the victims in this horrible affair?"

His tone was vibrant, sincere.

His eyes were aglow with pain and desperation.

"I don't have," said Me Susane, her gaze probably expressing, she told herself, the same pain, the same desperation, "I don't have the right to convince Marlyne about anything to do with you. That's not my place, surely you understand. It's not my job to do what you like. The only thing that can matter to me is my client's best interest. Is it in her interest for you to come visit her? That's the only thing I can consider, surely you understand."

"Yes, yes," said Principaux hopefully. "Because yes, try, I'm begging you, try to convince her she'll feel better if she gets a visit from me now and then, because we loved each other, because we loved each other very much, because I'm hurting, and I hurt less when I can see her."

He slapped the sides of his thighs, helpless, then, as if succumbing to weariness, letting the tears overflow, letting them roll down the deep creases between his nose and his cheeks.

"Because I'm hurting, Maître, because I'm hurting," he hiccupped.

Because we're hurting, Principaux, because we're hurting, Me Susane did not say to him.

The blood from her wound now seemed to be trickling inside her, not particularly painful, almost as if it were simply her period starting up.

Relieved, she gingerly touched her cheekbones, her eyebrows, underneath her eyes: no trace of eloquent moisture on her fingers.

She struggled to her feet.

She hobbled toward Principaux, put a hand on his shoulder, a fearful and reluctant hand, but one sure of its strength and legitimacy.

But who was Principaux to her?

Had there ever been any Majurauxs, any Ravalets?

Had there ever been, between her and all those names, anything at all?

She walked home that evening with tiny, labored steps.

Her knee was so swollen, viciously compressed by the cloth of her trousers.

The air was cold and damp, the pavement still icy.

Me Susane felt as if she were making no progress, as if her mischievous ankle boots were taking her back down the sidewalk when she ordered her feet to move forward.

She reached her door so despondent that, although she'd always condemned such profligacy, the bright glow of the lightbulbs turned on all over the apartment seemed to warm both her numb fingers and her pained, anxious heart, like a roaring fire in the hearth lit just for her by a friend, by a mother, by some caring soul.

Sharon came to meet her, followed by Lila, who was walking with a weird wriggle in her hips.

Surprised, Me Susane cried out:

"Why, Lila, I didn't know you were going to be here today, darling!"

Lila gave her a big smile, as was her habit with Me Susane.

"The papa came," explained Sharon, "he brought Lila, he had work to do. He thinks I take good care of her," Sharon added with a flush of pride that Me Susane found touching.

But she was still as startled as ever.

Why hadn't Rudy let her know?

"The papa won't be able to come pick up Lila tonight," Sharon went on. "He told me I should take Lila home with me and bring her back tomorrow."

"What, Sharon? On your bicycle? Really, he said that?"

Suddenly aware that her dismay might frighten Lila, on whose face she who knew the child so well could already see an expression more somber than usual, Me Susane forced herself to laugh, even with the pain in her knee becoming close to unbearable.

"I have a child's seat on my bike, obviously," said Sharon. "Sweetie, shall we be going?"

She tied the orange scarf around Lila's neck, the girl first reflexively resisting and then immediately giving in, defeated, Me Susane told herself, by Sharon's wise, resolute, quietly authoritarian tenderness.

Me Susane scarcely had time to give Lila a hug.

When she did, she smelled a strange odor on the little girl's neck—something sour, something frightened.

"Is everything OK, darling?" she whispered hurriedly.

The little girl answered with the enormous smile, at once warm, heartfelt, and impersonal, that she reserved, according to Rudy, for those she loved most.

And Me Susane let herself be convinced by that smile, dimly aware (but she was so tired, and in such pain!) that she was taking the coward's way out.

Once again, Sharon had made her a sumptuous dinner: rice pancakes stuffed with ground lamb and coriander, sautéed new potatoes with lots of garlic and parsley, a salad of chicory and red endive.

Not wanting there to be leftovers, Me Susane ate more than she would have liked.

Compulsively, often, she put her hand to the wound on her forehead, which she'd cleaned and disinfected, a ring of swollen flesh already forming around it.

She felt shocked, wronged, humiliated, as if someone had dealt her a terrible blow there, deliberately.

Once she'd finished her meal, she called Rudy.

"You didn't tell me you were bringing Lila over today."

"Well," said Rudy in a surprised voice, "I thought that was understood, that I could bring her over whenever I needed to, wasn't it? And I also asked Sharon to take Lila to sleep at her place tonight."

"Yes," said Me Susane. "Isn't that a little . . ."

Suddenly her mind went blank.

All her vocabulary deserted her.

What was she trying to say?

She hadn't the faintest idea.

"A little what?" asked Rudy defensively.

"A little . . . My knee hurts so much, you know, I fell down earlier today . . . A little premature, that's it."

"I don't think so," said Rudy slowly. "You told me you were sure Sharon would look after Lila perfectly."

"Yes," said Me Susane, "I'm not worried about that at all."

"Well then, my sweet, why should Lila not sleep at her nanny's? If it makes everyone happy?"

"Yes," said Me Susane, "yes."

She took a deep breath.

"Are you sure, Rudy, that Lila is happy? Did she tell you that in so many words?"

"Of course, it's obvious. Don't you think?"

"I don't like," said Me Susane firmly, "Sharon taking her to that other woman's apartment, the woman she cleans for, near the cathedral. We don't know that woman, after all."

"Lila made it clear that she's a very nice old lady, she only sees her for a moment, and she always stays close to Sharon. Everything seems perfectly fine to me, my love, I think you're getting worked up over nothing. Why is that, incidentally? It's not like you to worry for no reason . . . I'll be there tomorrow morning to pick up Lila. You don't have to be home, I'll see to everything with Sharon. That's what we agreed on, right?"

Her head churning, Me Susane couldn't recall coming to any systematic agreement with Rudy concerning Lila's care.

Had she forgotten?

Or was Rudy trying to impose his way on her?

"Well," she concluded, "as long as everything's good for Lila, that's the important thing, isn't it?"

She found herself carefully enunciating the words of that banal sentence, articulating them with an exaggerated clarity, as if, she thought in alarm, she were already making the case for her own innocence in a hypothetical trial to which all those who had not taken sufficient care of the vulnerable Lila would be summoned to testify.

The next day, she set off before Sharon and Lila came back.

She limped in her fleece-lined boots to the tram.

She had a feeling her knee had swollen in the night, so much so that she'd taken care not to look at it that morning, lest her anxious eye, her distracted attention, make it puff up even more.

She took the tram to the prison.

She felt, in Marlyne's account, the absence of something that intrigued and horrified her, something she would rather never hear, never know, but which she couldn't allow herself not to, if only so she could carefully avoid bringing it up at the trial: When exactly had Marlyne given in to the decision she'd made?

How had the idea taken on a reality in her mind?

And how long had she been thinking about it?

For an hour, or since the day before, or for months?

And what did she feel when the thought, the fantasy, the possibility of killing her children surfaced inside her?

Was it a flickering flame that her reason, her love could immediately snuff out?

Was it a raging fire she was glad she couldn't contain?

Where did her deadly thoughts take shape—in the bedroom, in the kitchen, on the way to the school?

Or was it perhaps certain images from her nightmares that had inspired her, swayed her, corrupted her, then convinced her that she had to make them concrete, that that was how she had to answer the command given her by her dreams?

How many times, in her youth, had Me Susane received orders to get even with the boy from Caudéran for the wrong that on waking she was no longer sure he'd done her, but which her dreams presented to her as something indisputable and awful!

Because her dreams suggested they knew more than she did, more and better, and that by obeying their exhortations to vengeance she would be relying on a justice far higher than society's justice, with its doubts, its delays, and also her waking self's justice, which, doubting, delaying, made her forget any thought of punishing the boy who might have been named Gilles Principaux.

But it wasn't Marlyne who walked into the little room where Me Susane was waiting, it was a warden, alone, bearing a message.

"She doesn't want to see you."

She handed the piece of paper to Me Susane.

"But leave me alone," it said.

"Can you tell her, please, that I'm waiting for her? That she has the right to change her mind and come talk to me? I'll stick around."

Me Susane took her computer from her fat satchel.

She opened an outraged email from her client who vehemently yearned to change his name, an answer to a letter she'd sent him expressing her fear that the authorities would see no legitimate grounds for his request since she herself, Me Susane, had found nothing to prove any ancestor of his had taken part in the slave trade, just as the name had never been listed by any of the associations that made it their work to unmask slave traders and demand that their names be removed from this or that street.

No street in Bordeaux had been given her client's name.

Did he, Me Susane had asked, wish to pursue his request?

To stay mired in his groundless obsession?

"I'm paying you to find something, you have to find something. That name is the name of an abomination, I know it is, I've heard things in my family. It's true, it's real, so there have to be records of it. I've devoted years of my life to this, and I'll never give up. I will not die with that ignoble name, it will not be engraved on my headstone. If we lived in a truly free country, the fact that I want it would surely be grounds enough, wouldn't it? What concern is it of the government's if I want a new name? I'm not despairing, but I am running out of patience. Keep looking, Maître! Something always turns up, the universe of the internet is infinite. I can't bear the thought that someone might one day spit on my grave. But I understand that person who will one day come and curse me. In my thoughts I spit on my name, and on the grave of my vile ancestor. All the same, I have no wish to be the target of that insult, because I don't deserve it, as you know, I'm fighting to rid myself of that disgrace."

Me Susane worked for a bit less than an hour, briefly nodded off.

She didn't know if she'd been roused from her slumber by a

fresh jolt of pain in her knee or the entrance of Marlyne Princi-paux, whom the warden brought into the room with a friendly wink in Me Susane's direction.

Marlyne grudgingly pulled out her chair, deliberately scrap-ing it over the concrete floor, like a sullen child.

Me Susane grimaced inwardly.

Her hand fluttered up to the wound on her brow, fleetingly caressed the rim, still painful but now perfectly dry.

It was an ugly gash, a lesion of no elegance, Me Susane had thought as she stood at her mirror that morning.

Shouldn't she have it looked at? she'd wondered, knowing perfectly well that she wouldn't, that she would always find specious reasons why she didn't have time.

Although she didn't say it to herself outright, she was dis-covering that she didn't mind showing herself to the world in that state.

But how could she dare face her parents again with that blot on her brow?

Marlyne was wearing the same sweatshirt as before.

Now it was spattered with grease spots.

She sat with her clenched fists in the ventral pocket, thighs firmly clasped on the metal chair.

Her pale yellow hair hung down her cheeks, which M^e Su-sane thought fuller than before, as if swollen by a regal, hostile self-assurance.

Her curt gaze landed on Me Susane's forehead.

"Well!" she puffed.

The shadow of compassion flitted through her gray-green eyes.

Me Susane couldn't help putting her hand to her forehead again.

She struggled out a smile.

"I fell down, it was icy."

"Quite a knock you took," said Marlyne, in a voice that Me Susane suddenly thought must have been her voice from before, charitable, considerate, friendly, the sweet voice of a diligent mother and an attentive teacher.

And Marlyne bent forward, as if to bandage Me Susane's pain by the radiant warmth of her flesh.

Then she brusquely sat up straight, and her manner was once again sullen, superior, almost aggressive.

"But I always knew my children wouldn't live to adulthood, but I always knew it but knowing it filled me with despair, but what I didn't know was that I would perform my act. But I thought some misfortune would strike them from outside, but that a car would run them down but that a fire would . . . But I had visions of catastrophes befalling them. But I sometimes woke with a start, but I'd dreamt they were dead and I'd done nothing to save them. But I never dreamt of them dying by my hand, but never but never. But that morning I was feeling very depressed. But I was thinking something was going to happen to my children but then what would I do without them? But all alone with Monsieur Principaux? But when I ran the bath I didn't really know anything was going to happen. But I was listening to a show about philosophy on France Culture but they were talking about Levinas but they quoted him: 'The face is what forbids us to . . .' But I liked that sentence but as you see but I still remember it. But the children weren't making any noise, they were good children but they were very careful around me but they hated seeing me sad but they loved me, I think. But they were afraid for me, but I think, yes. But Jason often asked me: Are you all right, Mama? But he sometimes asked me that ten times a day but always out of earshot of Monsieur Principaux, he would have been angry. Are you all right, Mama? But I can still hear his anxious little voice, but I can so clearly see his happy smile when I answered: I'm just fine, honey, but then I kissed him but then I kissed him many times in a day but he was never reassured for long but I think he sensed in me, it was like he was the grown-up, he sensed a turmoil, but yes a turmoil, a turmoil in my tormented mind and my bitter, bitter, bitter heart. But Jason understood me but he didn't die willingly I had to struggle with him but we wrestled in the cramped tub, clutching each other in the warm bathwater, which spattered and splashed. But when I got up that morning I didn't know I was going to do it. But like every day I knew my beloved children were going to be taken from me but I didn't know how or when but only that they would be and . . . But I hurried that moment along but I didn't have the right but I thought their passing would be less painful if it was me . . . But if it was me performing that act, but I who loved them and cherished them. But I knew it I knew it I knew we were destined for the most terrible sorrow. But I got up like every morning but like every morning my heart was heavy but no more or less than usual. But I gently poured water over Julia's head to rinse away the shampoo but I dipped the back of her head in the water to rinse it more quickly but the rest followed, her face, her neck, but then I couldn't go back and I knew the moment I'd been thinking of with horror ever since they were born had come but then I knew yes. But I thought but I thought there we are it's happened and sorrow has come to our house to stay. A great tranquility came over my soul because it had finally happened because I wouldn't have to dread it anymore since it had happened. But that's why, Maître, but that's why we mustn't blame anything on Monsieur Principaux."

Marlyne began to sweat profusely.

Me Susane reached out toward her, knowing that, from where she sat, she couldn't possibly touch her.

She saw her hand hovering in the air, trembling, fingers spread, between them.

Don't come any closer, someone who had walked into the room at that moment would have translated.

But was that what it was?

Nothing that Marlyne had said had yet touched, in Me Susane, the source from which understanding and pity suddenly begin to flow.

That woman, Me Susane vaguely thought, was not only someone she was sitting in front of but some*thing,* and that thing was still alien to her.

Not: Who is Marlyne? But: What is Marlyne? she asked herself, disoriented, all her anger at that woman subsiding.

When, somewhere toward noon, she went home, she was astonished to find that Lila was still there, or again there, with Sharon.

"The papa didn't come pick up Lila?"

"No," said Sharon merrily.

Still as buoyant as ever, she fixed her gaze on Me Susane's forehead.

Then, as if out of discretion, she looked away.

She was cheery, beaming, relieved.

Me Susane had never seen her this way.

She knelt down before Lila, who, sitting on a kitchen chair, seemed slightly changed from the day before, as if slighter, shrunken, not in the sense that that plump little girl had lost weight but as if her entire person had been lessened, reduced, crumpled.

A hint of a smile slightly twisted her mouth.

Me Susane held her close.

"Everything OK, sweetheart?"

Lila laid her damp forehead on Me Susane's wound.

A searing pain made Me Susane groan.

It felt as if her wound had burst into flames, fueled at once by that contact with Lila's forehead and by what the child was trying to get across to her.

At the price of a great effort, she gently pushed the girl away.

Such was her pain that she could have brutally tossed Lila aside, simply by reflex!

"Lila seems a bit funny," she whispered in Sharon's ear.

"Yes," Sharon chuckled, "Sweetie's funny, everyone likes her so much."

"Oh," said Me Susane hesitantly, "I'm sorry, I meant she seems strange, not like she usually is, don't you think?"

"Well," said Sharon after a silence, "Sweetie's in a good mood, she's happy to be with me. I don't know what she was like before. We're both happy, that's all."

She looked up at Me Susane, her gaze full of reproach, mistrust, and, almost, disgust.

"Did you go back to Madame Principaux's apartment?" Me Susane whispered.

Her blazing wound might have been bothering Sharon, making her face uncomfortably hot, so Me Susane took a prudent step back, taking care to go easy on her damaged knee.

"Yes," said Sharon, cold and circumspect. "The papa said it was a good thing."

Me Susane couldn't help raising her voice:

"I don't think, Sharon, that he said it was a good thing, I think he just said he didn't see anything wrong with it, unlike me. And, Sharon, tell me . . ."

Suddenly Me Susane's head began to spin.

She staggered to the living room, dropped into an armchair.

Sharon kept her distance, skeptical, deeply disapproving, as if watching some indecent, provocative performance in which she saw no artistic merit.

"Did Lila meet Madame Principaux today?" murmured Me Susane.

"She might have," Sharon answered cautiously. "Maybe she did see the old lady, I don't know. Sweetie likes to explore the apartment while I vacuum. She's a very nice old lady, very ordinary. You shouldn't worry."

In a pitying voice, she added:

"Where's the evil? That's what you're afraid of, but where is it? She's just an old lady who can't leave her apartment anymore, poor woman. That's not where you'll find evil lurking."

Sharon let out a quick, knowing laugh that Me Susane, who'd always naïvely thought of Sharon as a solid but essentially simple woman, reserved and deferential, was slightly stung to hear.

She couldn't help thinking that Sharon had always looked down on her from the height of her own respectability, by which standard, inexplicably, Me Susane, was no better than dirt.

Oh, she'd felt that so clearly!

And here was Sharon talking about something she manifestly knew how to identify, something that was in no way unknown to her, something impure and despicable that she seemed to know all about.

Why, then, could she not judge Me Susane with a compassionate eye?

And how could her practical knowledge of wickedness not have made it clear to her that Me Susane had to be protected?

Had to be kept on the side of honor, integrity, innocence?

Because Me Susane had never done wrong.

"No, madame, evil isn't there with her," Sharon went on, seething, "it doesn't live in that woman's apartment. You want to know where it lives? I'll tell you."

She raised her arm, a vindictive index finger pointing into the distance.

"Madame, evil's address is back on Mauritius, in my house. It's taken up residence there, and its . . . ramifications reach me even here, yes, madame. It's not enough to run away from them, you'd have to cut every tendril. That important paper, the one you've been asking about for months, it's being held prisoner back home, I'll never be able to set it free, that's how it is. Yes, madame, I know evil's address at this moment. It gets around, it can go wherever it likes. Just now it's staying in my house back home, it's happy there, and there's nothing to be done, everyone has to welcome it and show it a smiling face. So, yes, madame, I'm telling you, stop thinking about Madame Principaux, because you're wasting your time, her apartment is empty and as pure as any other and Sweetie's in no danger there!"

Sharon boldly raised her little head to underscore what she was saying.

She'd been speaking without looking Me Susane in the eye, only fixing her hands and shoulders with a hard, certain, slightly weary gaze.

The front door opened, and Rudy stepped into the hallway, calling Lila in a warm, tender voice.

"So," Me Susane asked herself, shocked, "so Rudy has a key now?"

She labored to her feet.

"Rudy!" she called out jovially, "I didn't know you had a key to my place!"

"Oh, you're here!"

He turned toward Me Susane, gave her a quick embrace.

She was steeling herself to explain how she'd gotten such a spectacular wound on her forehead, but since Rudy said nothing of it, seemed not even to notice, she held her tongue.

"You don't remember giving me your key?"

He seemed surprised, amused, teasing.

"I gave you my key?" murmured Me Susane.

"Well, of course you did! Quite some time ago, actually."

"And why would I do such a thing?"

She did her best to strike a casual tone, but a muffled, uneasy anger was pushing her to challenge Rudy—his smug, smirking face, indifferent and sly.

She had no memory of entrusting a copy of her key to Rudy, nor to anyone else but Sharon.

Why was he trying to deceive her?

"Well," said Rudy, suddenly serious, "you were thinking, and you were right, that it would simplify things, with Lila, that we could come and go more easily . . ."

"Lila didn't used to come here this often. She split her time between your mother and you, and every now and then she went to La Réole and stayed with my parents. I really cannot imagine," Me Susane repeated in a voice shriller than she would have liked, "why I would have given you my key."

"Well, you did, that's all!" Rudy exclaimed brightly. "And you know perfectly well that to Lila you're her only mama, her real mama! Isn't that right, darling?" he said in a singsong voice to Lila, who had come out of the kitchen (her little chair of memories) to greet him, her arms raised mechanically, her skin gray, her body pocked, hammered, her two black eyes as if pushed in, deep beneath the surface of her face.

How, Me Susane wondered in bewilderment, could she be the only one to realize the child wasn't at all well?

Rudy, who had always devoted an anxious, astute attention to Lila's feelings, an attention all the more discerning in that it was shot through with guilt, took her lovingly in his arms, as was his habit, but, Me Susane noted, he wasn't looking at her as he usually did when he put his big hands on Lila's shoulders, squatted on his heels, and roared in the ogre voice the child so loved, "When can I finally feast on this little lamb?

"Everything go OK?" he yelled toward Sharon, his voice excessively sunny.

"Yes," said Sharon with dignity (oh, her inflexible elegance, her natural propriety! Her instinctive reluctance to take part in a suspect merriment!). "Sweetie and my children got along fine. They all played together, and then they went to sleep at almost the same time."

"Oh, I'm so glad!" cried Rudy. "So, my little Lila, would you like to go back to Sharon's? Would that be fun for you, tell me?"

The little girl buried her face in Rudy's thigh.

She seemed to be trying to sink into it completely, to return to a peaceful and, if possible, endless gestation.

Rudy felt some unease at that, Me Susane thought she saw.

He gently pushed Lila away.

Why could he not accept that she felt a deep, intimate satisfaction in thinking she'd come from her father's reassuring thigh and nowhere else?

Since the mother was so unsteady, so dubious, so questionable!

Once Rudy and Lila were gone, Me Susane quickly downed the exquisite leftovers from Sharon's past meals (fried pork-and-rice meatballs, cabbage gratin, apple compote) while Sharon pretended to be busy cleaning the apartment.

Then, in the cold wind, in the cold, gloomy light of yet another afternoon of an endless winter, Me Susane left for her office and Sharon set off as well, forthright and self-assured, no longer hiding, to put in her daily hours at Madame Principaux's.

But she said nothing about it.

Mᵉ Susane was grateful to her for skipping the little ruse that leaving the apartment after her would have been for Sharon.

This way Sharon was no longer lying to her by omission.

She was forcing Mᵉ Susane to accept her way of leading her life, of organizing her work, and of earning money she sorely needed.

Sharon was no longer lying to her, there was no reason to, because her heart was august and because Mᵉ Susane now seemed to consent to everything that once aggrieved her.

She was so exhausted when she reached the office that she dropped into her armchair, dozed off, and so forgot all her pain (mangled knee, incandescent forehead).

The thin, imperious bell of an incoming text message made her start, so rarely did she get one.

Oddly (no, it wasn't odd, it was shocking, and it meant nothing good!), the message came from her father, Monsieur Susane, who had never once called on her cell phone or sent her a text, leaving that practice to Madame Susane out of a manly reticence, getting in touch only if there was reason for serious concern, delegating all superficial correspondence to his wife, though always subsequently coming to her for news.

Such that Mᵉ Susane had no memory of ever speaking to her father on the telephone, or ever once talking to him at home without Madame Susane being there.

. . .

"Adieu, my daughter, this is your father writing you, your mother doesn't know, has no need to know, or rather just now she needs not to know, so I'm counting on you not to tell her about this message. Adieu, my daughter, you've done us a great harm, without meaning to I think, and your mother is very upset, which upsets me terribly as well. She spends all her time trying to come up with a name. She wants to give you the name you're looking for but she can't, so she invents them. She doesn't know it, but she's inventing them, they come to her in dreams and then she throws them out to you as if they were real. Majuraux, Rava- let, another one that she told me and I've forgotten—something like Robineau, as you see, it's nothing short of ridiculous. She refuses to speak the name Principaux, having realized that Prin- cipaux is the name you want to hear, and she knows she would be bearing false witness if she gave in to your implicit request, almost your prayer—she knows she would be sating your hunger at the price of a senseless and dangerous lie: she knows no one by the name Principaux, and never has. Adieu, my daughter, your mother is losing her grip before my eyes. I can't let her fall, I can't let her be submerged. So adieu, my daughter, for this is the only way to save your mother. Do not ask her for another name, do not force her to remember who knows what things that probably never were, do not force her to satisfy you by constructing inside herself a horrible drama that she's beginning to take for real life. Adieu, my daughter, and be strong enough to make no attempt to contact us until tact, wisdom, and kindness have returned to you—particularly wisdom, from which all virtues flow."

E VERY MORNING THE SAME mysterious scraping sound pulled Me Susane from a simple, fortifying sleep, a sleep of exactly the right length, precisely filling the eight hours between her drifting off in this new bed and her waking to the sound of that scratching, that rustling, which came from outside and whose source she liked not trying to discover— what would be the point?

That enigmatic sound woke her at just the right time, when she'd slept all she wanted to sleep, and before venomous, sterile images could take advantage of her slumber to obliquely trouble her.

What was that scrabbling under her window?

Later, almost in spite of herself, she would learn that Christine, her landlady and the owner of the little grocery on the ground floor, took a hard, heavy broom to the courtyard pavement very early each morning, whereby there came to Me Susane's window the signal that it was time to get up, which she did with an eagerness she'd never known before, and an earnest impatience to plunge her convalescent body into the body of the city—invigorating, harsh, of no indisputable fineness or beauty—to which her strange illness had led her.

Even after Christine told her she swept the little courtyard behind the store very early each morning, Me Susane, gently extracted from her night, would go on wondering, happy and detached: Where could a sound like that come from, why do I not recognize it?

So much, here, would she enjoy suspending any reflex to reconcile what she knew with what she perceived, or what she wanted with what she was given—for instance, the breakfast she ate, by mutual accord, in the company of Christine and Ralph, which, as distant as could be from the things she liked to eat in the morning, with its spiced fritters, its over-strong tea, its mushy margarine, didn't please her at all and didn't matter to her either—all that was fine with her because this was how it was, and so she no longer concerned herself with her tastes or her preferences or, almost, her moral values: a relief.

She got up that March morning vaguely vowing to talk to Christine and Ralph, once breakfast was over, about what had brought her to their house.

Her room, already dear to her heart despite its frigid tiles and paltry furnishings—a varnished pine bed, a rickety little armoire, and a green plastic garden table—looked toward the east.

The white, sparkling morning light streamed in cold waves over the gray tiles, over the drab, bare walls, the flagrant shabbiness of the place, its open, indifferent ugliness.

Me Susane dressed, stood at the tiny bathroom's mirror,

tending to the still-oozing wound on her forehead, then sat down on the bed again, waiting for breakfast time to come.

She didn't want to upset her hosts by appearing even two minutes before the appointed hour.

She sensed in Christine and Ralph, despite their mercantile affability, a couple with rigorous ways, whom imprecision of any sort very likely offended and swayed toward a severe judgment of the person displaying it.

Not that Me Susane was particularly concerned with what her landlords thought of her.

But she couldn't help feeling, when she was with them (and her face, which she hoped was ardently honest, before theirs, which unquestionably were!), that she represented Sharon.

The ambassador of the proud, ambitious, irreproachable woman that was Sharon, the messenger of all those qualities and all that success, since Christine and Ralph never doubted that Sharon had "made good in her exile," had an obligation to be exemplary, impervious to any hint or thought of reproach.

It was thus Me Susane's duty to be one with Sharon, with the enviable, well-protected person, the victorious and perfectly armored person Sharon seemed to be for her brother and sister-in-law.

And so, sitting on her bed in the almost unendurable brightness of the sunrise streaming through the curtainless window, she sat watching the minutes go by on her phone.

Every now and again, fleetingly, her gaze landed on her feet, so pale that they seemed almost green under the straps of her flip-flops, on her strangely prominent knees, her narrow thighs—her own flesh, which she once knew so well and which she now had to work to recognize.

Wasn't it strange, she asked herself, that Sharon, that Rudy, that even Lila in her way, had a knowledge of her body that she herself lacked?

They'd clearly made Me Susane's poor body, her lost, ailing body, a site of attentive, intelligent care, anxious and thoughtful, and of a solicitude she wouldn't have thought possible without love for the personality housed in that body.

So did that mean she was loved?

At that thought, Me Susane began to tremble on her bed.

The blaze of the dawn slapped her forehead, reanimating, she thought, her suppurating wound and giving her, morning after morning, the same faint, intoxicating migraine.

She sat still, at once rapt, focused, and numb.

That feeling reminded her, not without a vague sort of pleasure, of what she'd felt before, in the previous weeks, when, bedridden in her Bordeaux apartment, clearly ill though stricken by no recognizable affliction, she perceived more than she saw the zealous, flitting comings and goings of an efficient, kindly Sharon and an equally energetic Rudy, a Rudy equally determined to pull her through.

The two of them floated around her bed like will-o'-the-wisps, nimbly cooperating for the sole purpose of caring for and watching over Me Susane, whose mind was wavering, whose body was flagging.

They whispered to each other, and she never once thought they were conspiring.

On the contrary, she sensed that they were communicating

the information most likely to rid her of the hurt that was inhabiting her.

In her confusion, Me Susane imagined herself bound for life to that hurt, while those two unexpected guardians, those familiar saviors, seemed to have taken it on themselves to free her from it.

There is no burden, no grief, no injury of which we cannot, by our loving will, deliver you, those two silhouettes' discreet ballet told her as they fluttered around her.

Once she called out for her parents, but her cry only awoke a new pain, since Monsieur and Madame Susane had by all appearances written her off.

"They won't come, my darling," Rudy told her gently.

But what did he know?

Had he read the message from her father?

Had he got his hands on her phone?

Even if he had, how could he be so sure that Monsieur and Madame Susane, all discord set aside and the Principaux question temporarily forgotten, would not rush to answer the call of their unhappy, bedridden daughter, their only child, suddenly laid low by the sorrow of living?

She thought she heard herself asking Rudy: Would you mind trying to get hold of them all the same?

She couldn't make out if she was speaking in a dream or in reality, if Rudy couldn't understand her or if he'd pretended not to hear for her own good and because he knew from a mysteriously reliable source that Me Susane's parents wanted nothing more to do with her.

And so she tossed and turned, the usually restrained voices

of her inner self suddenly howling but bringing no trace of relief—pointless rage, piteous, sterile indignation.

A welcome drowsiness swallowed up all those questions.

She would drift off, then wake up in a different mood, confident, fatalistic.

Rudy was wiping her face with a damp, soft cloth, warm and perfumed.

She liked to think it was that fragrance that woke her (lily of the valley? lilac?) and not Rudy's delicate fingers on her cheeks, her forehead, the corners of her mouth, the wings of her nose—so kindly, so attentive were those fingers that she felt crushed by a sadness she'd never known.

Because, back when he loved her, did Rudy ever show her such kindness?

Or maybe he did, and she'd done her best not to see it?

Now, sitting on her new bed in the blaze of the early morning, how far away seemed the evening when she came home from the office after reading Monsieur Susane's message!

She felt a torpor come over her.

She sat up straight, checked the time: What would they think of her, and collaterally of Sharon, if she was late for breakfast?

Although downing a big meal at sunup did her no good, brought her neither pleasure nor benefit, she'd come to like joining Christine and Ralph at the severe table of their little kitchen in the back of the shop, none of them speaking save to pass the margarine or the pepper.

Ralph, Sharon's brother, had her pale gray eyes and her little face, a face minimized as if out of ingrained frugality—no need-less expanse of skin, thin cheeks, narrow brow, invisible chin, the nose short, the mouth well-shaped but small.

Christine, his wife, who'd intimidated Me Susane from the start, stood up straight and strong, and her whole being, dense and ample, packed with a hard, restrained, vigorous flesh, her cold eyes, her stoical air, ruled out any possibility that Me Susane might win her over with her own virtues—her convalescent state, her title, her friendship with Sharon.

Christine clearly was not the type to be taken in.

Me Susane, who was here to persuade them, or in some just or unjust way to take from them what they justly or unjustly wanted to keep, mentally surrendered to Christine's curt incorruptibility, even if that virtue was grounded in an indelicacy or a betrayal.

Had she brought herself into their house to convince them or to deceive them?

To make them see reason or to put one over on them?

Did she, come to that, still know how to do either one, to convert or to dupe?

Sitting on her new bed and scrupulously eyeing the passing time on her phone, Me Susane began to doubt everything she'd ever known about herself.

Her memory of the few weeks Sharon and Rudy had spent caring for her was hazy, but she recalled with almost infuriating precision her desperate return home after leaving her office, locking the door, and telling herself she would never go back, that she had none of the qualities of a respectable lawyer, that even her parents, the only people on earth who loved her unconditionally, were now passing the cruelest but surely the most accurate judgment on her: she'd failed in every way.

There was no one she hadn't let down.

Including the young Principaux or Majuraux or Ravalet in the Caudéran house, whom, she abruptly remembered as she locked her office door, she'd disappointed in some way that her memory couldn't summon—all at once she pictured him, the young man she'd surprised with her words, with the brilliance of her desperate intelligence, she saw him pointing disdainfully toward the door, the door to that wonderful bedroom he'd allowed her to know and from which he'd scornfully expelled her, she couldn't recall why.

But what did come back to her, violently, suddenly, was her awareness of the boy's displeasure, the profound aversion she'd caused without meaning to.

What had she done in that room to merit that boy's disgust, and her conjecturing father's?

Wasn't there a contradiction there?

What she'd done could have pleased the boy and offended the father, or disappointed the boy and relieved the father, but how could it be that she'd attracted the enmity of them both, the long-ago young man waving her out of the room and the present-day father banishing her from the loving realm of the Susane family, her father who'd seen nothing, who knew nothing, and who was now chasing after chimeras?

But if there was a contradiction, wasn't that her fault?

What innocence could she proclaim when, all thanks to her, her own father was cobbling together painful fantasies and her mother was inventing names for the guilty parties?

And that boy in Caudéran, what would he have to say of the child she was, there in his room, who, possibly, had trapped him in the snare of a brilliant display that was frantic, yes, but no less overpowering and corrupting?

What would he accuse her of today, perhaps justifiably?

Me Susane came home to her apartment in a state of deep emotional fragility.

She quickly undressed and fell into bed, and her knee hurt and the wound on her forehead seemed to be slowly devouring her entire face.

She burst out in sobs, great gushes of tears and mucus that filled her with dismay.

Oh, is that me crying like this, and why, and what good does it do?

She was still weeping when Sharon came in, humming as she turned on all the lights, then serenely noticing that Me Susane was there.

"There now, there now," she murmured.

With a hand as practical and efficient as it was soothing, she washed Me Susane's face, hands, and feet, bathed them in a way Me Susane would forever find miraculous.

Because with that the source of her sadness ran dry.

And Sharon brought her a spiced chicken bouillon, so quickly conjured up that it seemed to have sprung from the sheer performative force of her will.

Me Susane then slipped into a strange sleep.

Even as she slept, she knew she was sleeping, knew she was distantly participating in the things going on around her.

So she felt the presence of Rudy and Lila, of their two bodies just in from the frigid city, radiating the strange smell of cold perspiration and the equally powerful odor of their concern.

They were worried about her!

Rudy was tenderly pulling the comforter up to Me Susane's cheeks, just as she liked it, and Lila was laying a furtive hand on her lacerated forehead, setting off a shudder of pain but at the same time a surge of gratitude, as Lila was manifestly the only one who'd noticed Me Susane was wounded.

When she emerged from the limbo of her sleep and spoke to Rudy or Sharon, she couldn't tell whether she was speaking out loud or within herself, nor whether they heard her or, humoring her, only pretended to.

The first thing she thought she'd said involved Lila.

"Don't let her go to Madame Principaux's anymore, never let Sharon take her there again!"

As she remembered it she was pleading, her torment and turmoil returning, and Rudy reassured her:

"Don't worry, everyone Lila spends time with is safe, and remember I've been taking care of my child from the beginning."

"But you don't know the Principauxs, you might think they can be trusted, and they probably can't!" objected Me Susane.

But could he hear her?

In any case, how much of all that did he understand?

He was in the dark.

He didn't know what she knew, what she sensed.

She, at least, could see, even emerging with a mind clouded from her slumbers in the murky depths, that Lila had changed.

And, she grumbled in her half dreams, don't try to tell me it's her puberty coming on.

Lila had the petrified, clenched face, a face as if veiled in indifference, of a child in pain, Me Susane was horrified to see from the bed of her own terrors.

Her bed in Port Louis was the bed of a rebirth.

So she mused, bathed in light, religiously awaiting her burdensome breakfast.

She was going to see Christine and Ralph again, and she had to make out what she was to them: a villain or a peace-bringing angel?

She liked that industrious, ascetic, solitary couple—or were they evil, as Sharon thought?

Puritans whose seemingly malevolent actions had to be measured by the standards of their own moral system, which made those actions coherent, necessary, perhaps even salutary.

And then no accusation of evil could hold up.

The alarm on her phone wrenched Me Susane from her watchful meditations.

She hurried to her feet.

She soundlessly left her room, brisk and muffled in her flip-flops, like Christine and Ralph, who, though they lived, spoke, and slept in a room separated from her by nothing more than a partition, never forced her to feel or remember their presence.

And even if their breath must sometimes have mingled with hers through minuscule interstices in the partition, tiny gaps offering passage to microscopic insects, Me Susane never heard them.

She was cohabiting with a pair of souls.

Let's hope, she said to herself, that they suspect the same of me! Let's hope they see me as nothing more than a *force*!

In a transport, she'd promised Sharon:

"I won't come home empty-handed."

Ordinarily distant, Sharon had taken her in her slender arms, pressed her brow to Me Susane's chin, and murmured:

"Yes, I know. In any case, if you don't succeed you won't come home at all."

Me Susane clearly remembered the moment when she realized, when she understood, when she learned the direction her desperate desire to exert a positive force on a bad situation had to take.

No doubt assuming she was asleep, Sharon and Rudy were on their way out of her room after airing it, cleaning it, straightening it, when Sharon spoke to Rudy in (thought Me Susane) a falsely offhand voice of the marriage certificate she couldn't get hold of, and which Me Susane so insistently demanded.

"But there's nothing I can do about it," Sharon said with a shrug. "There are two people hanging on to it. They don't want to send it to me. What can I do?"

Sharon, you can talk directly to me! Me Susane had silently cried out before reasoning with herself, suddenly very calm: What's the point, since I heard every word she said?

And then, just as placid, almost serene, this illumination: I've got to go and get that piece of paper.

And the fact that Sharon, when Me Susane informed her of her sudden, fervent resolution, seemed simply to have expected it, counted on it, proved to Me Susane that Sharon had realized it before she did.

"Yes, of course," said Sharon. "That's the only way. I don't know if we'll ever see you again. There's nothing else to be done. If not, one day or another, I'll be sent home with my husband and the children. You're going to save us.' "

Sitting up very straight facing Christine and Ralph at the breakfast table, Me Susane couldn't repress a smile as she remembered Sharon's words, although at the same time, deep inside, she was intimidated and trembling and more anxious to win them over honorably than she was determined to hoodwink them.

She was intrigued by Sharon's portrayal of those two, her brother and sister-in-law, whose faces Me Susane saw before her as if sculpted out of pure decency and respect for the law.

Sharon had gone so far as to slander them:

"They're a couple of thugs," she'd claimed with an unusual vehemence. "They're holding my papers hostage. They want me to die of sadness and jealousy. My husband's already dying of anxiety, he's lost all faith in himself, they've stolen his power and courage. They're murderers, in my own family, I can't love my brother anymore, or trust him. They're villains, yes, they're no good."

How, Me Susane wondered, discreetly studying her hosts, could two faces so forthright, so civil, and so prim be the faces of bandits?

She still didn't quite understand what sort of office Ralph went to after breakfast, but she now had a precise idea of the activities that made up Christine's workday in the shop, starting at seven in the morning.

She remembered certain insinuations that Sharon had made concerning her sister-in-law's regrettable dreaminess, and even her laziness, "letting the days drift by," as Sharon put it, to the detriment of that modest couple's necessary advancement toward a more comfortable life.

"She doesn't do much" was the laconic judgment of a Sharon proud of her own inexhaustible vigor.

When in fact Christine worked so hard!

Me Susane sent Sharon a stern rebuke in her thoughts.

Didn't you see, Sharon, back when you lived here, how early she gets up, how late she goes to bed, how quickly she eats lunch, and how, all on her own, very properly, very efficiently, she manages this little grocery store, which furthermore doubles as a café? You of all people, Sharon, you who know from experience the meaning of toil, could you have seen even the slightest idleness in Christine, even the tiniest trace of sloth?

Who was Principaux to her?

What was the Principaux family's real name?

Although visibly struggling against her preference for or habit of secrecy, against her submission to it or the impenetrable awareness of her duty toward it (toward sacrosanct secrecy), Sharon had finally consented to offer Me Susane a few details or episodes of her life in Port Louis, her stay with Christine and Ralph, her elders by six or seven years, when she lived, Me Susane inferred with some emotion, in this same room, slept in this same hard bed, and woke up each morning inundated by this same triumphant light.

Telling her story, Sharon had, deliberately or not, left the chronology hazy.

Me Susane couldn't say if Sharon lived with her brother before or after she met her husband, if the husband lived there as well, if the brother and husband even knew each other, and in a general way Sharon's telling left in the shadows everything she thought inessential to Me Susane's mission, not so much out of a desire for privacy or discretion or fear of boring her as to grant Me Susane only a meager affection, only a cautious, strategic show of friendship.

What Me Susane got from those few measured words, measured both in number and in meaning, was that Sharon and her brother Ralph were once very close, loved each other dearly in their tender youth (their father was a mason, their mother a homemaker), and were then divided by the choices they made as adults, or the misfortunes they suffered, and probably something else as well, which Sharon kept carefully hidden.

In any case, there was distance, bad blood, anger, and sorrow.

Me Susane thought it safe to assume that neither Christine nor Sharon's husband was responsible for that discord, that brutal, utter disharmony, they were outsiders, it wasn't their fault that the brother and sister had fallen out, it was above all the decision to emigrate to France that had separated them and locked them both away in an oppressive, spiteful silence.

Ralph very clearly found Sharon's wish to exile herself strange, presumptuous, and foolhardy.

Sharon was working as a maid in a luxury hotel where her husband, or the man who would become her husband, was employed as a gardener, or as a handyman, or as a caretaker for the exotic birds—parakeets, canaries, parrots—whose filigreed cages decorated the hotel's public spaces, or perhaps as an assistant in the kitchens, Me Susane couldn't be sure.

What she believed she did know was that Ralph considered the life Sharon and her husband had made for themselves through hard work and persistence an objectively adequate one.

They'd found safe harbor on the shores of a reasonable happiness, thought Ralph, according to Me Susane, and they were wrong to wager the whole of that humble felicity on the vague hope of an opulent life far from home, where they would never find light, eloquence, and sincerity again.

But Sharon, thought Me Susane, would hear no talk of a life that was simply good enough.

Unlike her brother, who could be happy within the limited range of his leaps and sprints, she had children she didn't want to see bounding about in a cramped cage, or any sort of cage for that matter, which seemed to anger Ralph, almost to insult him, and he assured her that in exile her children would grow up in a pen even more overt, even more confined.

Those two beautiful children Sharon had cautiously kept away from Me Susane!

And Sharon, a stubborn, stamping little goat, had stood up to her reasonable, dully practical brother, she'd gone off to France and then, once she'd set up camp, taken the necessary steps to have her husband and children come join her, at which, as Me Susane understood it, Ralph was still angry.

Sharon had blurted out something like:

"He'd gotten too attached to my children, what am I supposed to do about that? They're mine, not his, I certainly wasn't going to just let him keep them."

She might actually have said only a third of those words, Me Susane admitted to herself, but that was how she'd interpreted Sharon's cry of protest: Ralph, the beloved and infertile brother, would never forgive her for taking away his silkenhaired, honey-faced niece and nephew.

Which is why he was holding on to the paper, the marriage certificate that for months Sharon had been begging or ordering him to send her.

"He was hoping I'd come for it myself," Sharon had whispered anxiously, "and then, bang, he would hold me prisoner in their house, his and Christine's, and I wouldn't even know it, and time would go by and I'd work in the shop and I'd go to sleep, I'd forget about myself and even the children back in France, poof, forgotten. With you there's nothing they can do, they won't dare talk you into staying."

Ralph asked Me Susane if she wanted another cup of tea.

The white, fresh light from the well-swept little courtyard lit the otherwise dark kitchen, cold and tidy with its pale green walls, its deep brown wooden table, its lawn chairs whose hard metal slats pained Me Susane's backside.

Ever since she'd gotten here, almost two weeks before, she had the impression that her hosts' days were governed by a single-minded mission to show neither pleasure nor displeasure in any activity at all, for no matter the circumstance, whenever she met them or simply caught an unnoticed glimpse of one or the other they were invariably neutral, laconic, coolly composed, as if, thought Me Susane, they knew they were being watched by the terrible eye of Providence, which likes nothing so much as to punish the happy, the proud, the content.

But could they fool a potentially vengeful fate with a show of indifference and disinterest if their hearts were scheming, fearing, sometimes bleeding?

Sharon accused Ralph and Christine of focusing their thoughts on her to the point of obsession.

Their fevered imaginings pursued her even in France.

I can hear them sometimes, they want to capture my will, Sharon had whispered at Me Susane's bedside.

Or had she dreamt that?

She couldn't sort out what Sharon had said to her from words she only thought she'd heard from her lips.

Nonetheless, she was reassured by a private conviction that she made a good spokesperson for Sharon's vaguely expressed feelings, and even feelings never expressed at all but that Sharon had managed to mutely convey over the course of those days when, racked by despair, limp in her bed, and sick with sadness, Me Susane felt her soul permeable to any unspoken sorrow.

How could Rudy not see that something horrible was happening to Lila?

"Yes, thanks, I'd be glad of a touch more tea," she said in her most dignified voice.

Ralph filled her mug to the brim with that strong, black, fetid drink Me Susane despised—a poisonous tea, an incomprehensible, humus-tasting brew.

But she never said no to anything offered by her hosts, neither the very salty, oily biscuits Christine baked in the earliest morning, having made the dough before she went to bed, nor the slices of salami laid on those biscuits as soon as they came out of the oven, nor the canned fruit salad, too sweet and cloying to Me Susane's taste.

For Sharon's sake, she thought it essential to make the best possible impression on these two, even if that food so jangled her internal machinery that after breakfast she had to go upstairs and lie down in her floodlit room.

Sharon once lived in that room, and many tourists had passed through it as well.

"They rent out my room, you can stay as long as you like," Sharon had volunteered, her tone almost joking, perhaps sarcastic.

Either she meant that she didn't for one moment imagine Me Susane would feel like a long stay in that house, or else, on the contrary, she was teasing Me Susane on her good luck, the chance to combine work and a dream vacation, a mission (rescuing Sharon) and an ideally restful convalescence.

Living with Ralph and Christine demanded certain efforts that, although it pleased her to take them on, sapped a palpable part of Me Susane's strength.

Here she had to avoid any spontaneity in her words, had to rein in or even silence any outspokenness.

The room wasn't expensive.

Her hosts were hard and pure.

The money had been come up with.

Me Susane firmly pushed her thoughts aside whenever they came back to that.

But it was a fact, the money had been come up with.

One murmur from her that she couldn't afford such a trip and Rudy, back at her side, an ever-reliable presence like Sharon, and, more discreet but still trembling and afflicted, Lila, had reassured her with a single sentence:

"Don't worry, your parents and I have already seen to that."

And so Me Susane learned or concluded that Rudy had arranged things with La Réole, not asking her opinion, and the money for the plane and the room had been found.

By sending her so far away, were Monsieur and Madame Susane sending her to the devil?

Did they hope that, from a pleasant hell, she would never come back to them?

That morning Me Susane drained her second cup of tea at one go.

She boldly plunged her gaze into Ralph's unruffled eyes while Christine, in a hurry to get to work, to, as she said, "start her day," cleared the table, took the cup from Me Susane's hands, efficient, mutely conversing with herself, almost impudent in her vivacity.

Ralph was about to stand up when Me Susane reached out to lightly touch his arm.

He flinched, then reflexively rubbed at the spot where her fingers had grazed his skin.

But he was looking at her with a curiosity not devoid of kindliness.

"Sharon asked me for something," Me Susane began.

"Yes," said Ralph. "She's my only sister. May she live a long and joyful life."

"She asked me," Me Susane very gently went on, "to bring her back a document."

Christine, standing at the sink, suddenly stopped washing the cups and plates.

She kept her back turned, though listening, thought Me Susane, with her whole body.

"Yes," said Ralph amiably, "what kind of document?"

"Her marriage certificate. She needs it in France."

"Fine," said Ralph.

Me Susane thought she sensed a slight surprise in him.

Christine then turned to face them, tense, powerful, forcing her face to express only the vaguest of interests.

Her tone idly curious, she asked Ralph:

"Did you know they were married?"

"Yes and no."

"That's fine."

She looked relieved.

She rinsed the dishes, set them in the rack, her mind once more not on her task but on all the tasks to come, all the chores she'd have to do in the course of her day, no doubt considering, thought Me Susane, the most efficient order in which to take them on.

"Sharon," Me Susane continued in that same gentle voice, "has asked you many times to send her that document. Apparently you never answered?"

Ralph shrugged.

He gave her a forced smile, as if buying time to process his own surprise and then disguise it from Me Susane.

"She never asked me for anything," he said coldly. "She never calls. Maybe she's married, maybe she isn't. May she succeed beyond all her dreams."

"May she succeed!" exclaimed Christine as she stood at the sink, in a deep, vibrant tone.

"So you don't have the paper?"

Ralph had stood up, now resolved not to let a coaxing hand waft toward his arm and hold him back.

Me Susane didn't try to hide her astonishment.

"You really don't have it?" she asked again, absurdly.

"There's no way I could have it. Tell me, why would I have it? How much of all this actually exists? May Sharon's children live happy lives in their new country. Now I have to go to work, or I'll be late for the first time in my career."

He gave her a brief, brisk bow, his torso corseted in a tight white shirt, then hurried out of the kitchen.

"May Sharon's children . . ." Christine half sang in a distracted voice.

Demoralized, Me Susane felt a violent surge of rejection aimed at Sharon.

If she reflexively found Ralph credible, if she placed her faith in that stranger rather than in Sharon, whom she'd thought she knew a little, it was because deep down Sharon didn't like her, maybe even loathed her, and for that reason felt no compunction about telling her a lot of nonsense, oh, not with any goal or strategy in mind, simply out of disdain.

And, having lost faith in Sharon, Me Susane began to hate her.

She wished she could avenge herself by despising her even more utterly than Sharon very obviously despised her, though she knew she couldn't, that she would now forever be slowed, on the downhill slope of bitterness and rancor, by the selfless, thoughtful, almost friendly competence with which Sharon had cared for her in Bordeaux.

But in that case what to make of all this?

Why was Sharon so cavalierly toying with Me Susane's life?

Her fingers trembled on the screen of her phone when, back up in her room, she called her.

Sharon answered immediately, catching Me Susane off guard, and she whispered so that Christine, still busy in the kitchen just below her, wouldn't overhear what they were saying.

She'd expected Sharon to reject or ignore her call, to reject or ignore it forever, for all time!

"Sharon, I've just been speaking with your brother, he doesn't have the document, he doesn't even seem to understand what you're talking about."

Sharon said nothing.

The silence was so long that Me Susane could feel its texture.

Shaken, she had to accept that she'd insulted Sharon.

"Sharon, tell me, how is Lila?" she breathed imploringly.

"She's just fine. She's doing just fine, yes. She's a little girl," Sharon consented to answer after a few interminable seconds of offended reticence.

She added:

"The paper is in their bedroom dresser. You can't trust what my brother, Ralph, says, you know. I understand him, because I'll always love him. But sometimes his judgment isn't good. You're forcing me to say this, I don't like to criticize him. I love him, because I always understand him. As for Lila, she's just a little girl, you know. She's fine, she's not fine, it changes, that's how it is. That paper, Madame Susane, I know where you'll find it: in the dresser."

"Sharon, I can't go rooting around in their room!"

She let out a dismayed little laugh.

She put her hand to her forehead, her scar suddenly stinging again.

"Sharon, tell me something reasonable and acceptable I can do!"

"That's up to you. I don't know about these things. You're the one who promised."

"Not exactly!" Me Susane exclaimed, although Sharon had already hung up.

Not long after, she was walking in the street as she did every morning, but a nagging wariness, a muffled mistrust of herself, marred the pleasure she usually found in strolling through the neighborhood.

With a smile and a nod, she greeted Ralph and Christine's neighbor, who was unlocking his shop's steel shutter—a tobacconist who ever since she arrived had shown her an eloquent but discreet and courtly goodwill, making a little bow the moment he spotted her and at the same time avoiding her eye.

Me Susane's vision, that morning, was blurry.

She took off her sunglasses, put them on again, took them off.

She was stumbling in her flip-flops.

Her light trousers and loose blouse seemed to cling to her skin even though the temperature was far from warm at this hour.

The illness that had stricken her in Bordeaux had left her thinner, somehow unsteady (no doubt her father wouldn't think she looked like a man anymore, Me Susane told herself bitterly).

She was long and tapered, strangely narrow, she wobbled in her flat sandals as if she were wearing high heels, and she felt lessened, impoverished.

A power had left her, a power she hadn't recognized when she had it, a power that had alarmed Monsieur Susane.

Long before, Monsieur Susane had become afraid.

And when he did, she was ashamed that she'd lost her beauty in her father's eyes.

Now she missed the sturdiness that once was hers, the abundant, hard flesh that once wrapped her up, as if clasping her shoulders, her knees.

She mechanically crossed the street, not knowing where she was going, not caring.

A frigid breeze from the mountains, from the sharp green summits, skimmed over the pavement.

Her sweat turned cold on her calves.

Was she here so she would suffer even more?

Or so that Lila, now so far away, would suffer with no one to rescue her?

Unable, with her limited life skills, to call her to her aid?

Me Susane had never met Lila's mother, or if she had she didn't remember it—never, though, since Lila's birth, was she not certain that she could interpret the little girl's sibylline confidences better than anyone.

Rudy himself had not been initiated.

He looked after his beloved daughter, but he'd never approached her silence, didn't know there was one, accepted Lila concretely, tenderly, in the unquestioning style of the times.

Only Me Susane understood that Lila could not decently enter the home of Madame Principaux.

What was she doing, then, wandering the streets of Port Louis, feeling the mountains' unfriendly breath on her ankles, sensing that Lila, from whom she'd perhaps been carefully distanced, was paying Madame Principaux visits that plunged her into distress?

And into shame?

But, thank goodness, that was an emotion Lila probably had no access to.

Or maybe she did, maybe it was inborn, and Me Susane hadn't thought to watch out for it, deceived by the little girl's rudimentary personality?

How to know?

Shouldn't she be back home protecting Lila, not here trying to serve the interests of a Sharon who, for abstruse reasons, would never like her?

She walked into a little supermarket she recognized as the one she went to each morning to buy something for midday.

She'd thought she was wandering through unexplored streets, but she was only following her usual course, confined in a prudent perimeter around her lodgings.

The newly returned pain in her forehead fueled her fevered state, as did the dizzying sense that she'd had an inspiration: the person she should be rescuing from misfortune, from disgrace, from lonely sorrow, was not Sharon but Lila.

Oh, hadn't she got the wrong martyr?

The one she had a mission to save, wasn't it actually . . .

She quickly bought grated carrots and vacuum-sealed ham, exchanged a few words with the cashier, hurried out into the street, where the same cold wind immediately clasped her calves even as her face felt as if it were roasting, exposed to the enormous, fierce sun now awakening.

She walked as quickly as she could.

She had to go home at once.

But go home where, where would it be useful, appropriate, and as painless as possible to go?

To Sharon's brother's, or back to her apartment in Bordeaux, or to Monsieur and Madame Susane's, who couldn't have forgotten that not long before she was still their cherished daughter, the only offspring they would ever have?

Or maybe to Rudy's, since he was Lila's father and Me Susane would never have any progeny in this world but that helpless little girl—and what tenderness she felt for her!

Lila was her beloved child, whatever that might mean.

How could she not have fully realized that?

And abandoned Lila to the foolish hands of a father incapable of catching the scent of and then localizing a profanation— a father *who has no eye for evil*?

What had Sharon said about that?

That Me Susane had gotten *the wrong address*?

She stopped walking as she tried to remember.

Chilled by the mountains' breath, she'd lost all feeling in her ankles and feet, while, gripped in a strange sort of torment, her forehead, cheeks, and nape were bathed in sweat.

What Me Susane feared, the source of all wickedness, had temporarily taken up lodgings with Ralph and Christine, according to Sharon, and not with Madame Principaux.

She'd said something of that sort, yes.

Was she trying to lead her astray?

To send her to Port Louis so she herself could take Lila to the Principaux woman's lair every day with no questions asked?

Mistrustful though she was, Me Susane hesitated to go that far—although?

She turned back toward her room.

Her head churning, she lay down on the bed, her only thought to rest—and to warm her calves and cool her face.

Below her, she faintly heard Christine coming and going, she'd opened her shop, and now she was already serving her regulars their coffee.

How, as a child, Me Susane loved to hear Monsieur and Madame Susane bustling about in the morning, discreetly so they wouldn't wake her, in that cramped kitchen where they silently sipped at their mugs of strong coffee and then, at a very precise hour, an hour calculated to let Me Susane rest as long as possible without their then having to rush her, one of them would come into her little room, stroke her forehead, sweetly pretending to believe she was still asleep!

Me Susane woke up with damp cheeks.

She'd had a sad dream, to her great surprise.

And above all, which she hadn't been planning on, she'd fallen asleep.

It had always troubled her that she could produce melancholy reveries in her sleep but never dreams that might tell her, if only by way of countless mental ricochets, the things she wanted to know.

She'd seen her parents and the house in La Réole, and she'd gotten nothing from it.

Why did the clarity of her nocturnal visions never apply itself to Principaux, to the house in Caudéran?

Down at heart, she got out of bed.

Lying on the mattress was a piece of paper that she accidentally sent falling to the floor.

She hurried barefoot down to the shop.

Christine had just finished checking out a customer who cast a disapproving eye at Me Susane—her stunned, sweating face, her tousled mop of hair?

Christine was little more welcoming, her features seemed to freeze into a stiff, instinctive dignity inversely proportional to the turmoil and fervor, the disarray and disturbing ardor she must have thought she saw in Me Susane.

Me Susane stood up straight.

She pretended to try to smooth her bristling hair, caressed it with a diplomatic, reassuring hand—the ugly hair that had so saddened her father!

"Thank you," she forced out. "On behalf of Sharon, I mean."

"Fine," said Christine, in a tone that meant: "Let's hear no more about it."

"Ah!"

Me Susane, disappointed but stubborn and curious, raised her arms, palms up, with an insistent little smile.

And with that Christine exploded:

"We didn't have that piece of paper!" she cried. "Ralph found it somewhere, he went to a lot of trouble. He said farewell to his sister and the children, he'll never see them again, and if he did he wouldn't recognize them and they'd feel nothing for him. They're dead to his love, to his tenderness. He asked me if we could remember that paper, find it or rediscover it or even make one, and I said all right, let's be done with it. Then Sharon will never ask anything from us again. You'll see, she'll forget all about us now that she has no reason to talk to us. She got what she wanted, and it's not very pretty. I never curse anyone, as a matter of principle and prudence. But that ridiculous piece of paper will bring her nothing good."

Christine turned her head to take a deep breath in private.

The rippling flesh on her nape was trembling slightly.

"So that paper," Me Susane said softly, "wasn't in your bedroom dresser?"

Christine whirled around.

"Not at all! Ha ha! It wasn't anywhere, Ralph has suffered enough now, so stop. Myself, I don't say Blessed be Sharon! May grace be bestowed on those of us who like what we have and don't try to have what doesn't like us. Blessed be Ralph the steadfast!"

She applauded her own words with an air of desperate sarcasm.

Her hands clapped together, furious, sharp.

"But in that case," Me Susane murmured, "where does this paper come from?"

"Nowhere!" growled Christine. "Sharon dreamt, she demanded, she has her reward. I would never have gratified her with anything at all, only with my silence. But Ralph loves her, she's his little sister, and there we are, he did what he had to do to bring that sacred document to light. She sent you here, Ralph is answering her, he's giving in to her, and also he doesn't want you to have come here for nothing, because he respects you."

That evening Me Susane stood on the sidewalk watching for the taxi that would take her to the airport.

Night had just fallen, a mellow night, dark and warm.

Her suitcase at her feet, Me Susane kept the strap of the purse slung over her shoulder firmly clasped between her breasts.

A vague stench of sour milk emanated from the unpeopled, silent street.

But a jubilant fire was burning merrily in Me Susane's heart.

And how happy, against all her own expectations, she was to be going home!

Although the neighborhood was deserted and the unstirring air magnified every sound, she didn't see the attack coming.

All at once he was behind her, giving off no odor, making no sound.

He put his arms around her, tried to throw her to the ground, or rather, as it seemed to her, strangely, to lower her to earth, defeating her without pain.

He encircled her shoulders, trying to bend her, and his firm, assured grip was almost gentle, as if, Me Susane thought vaguely but quickly, he had no doubt she would submit, as if he didn't think it necessary to add an unwholesome violence to the inevitable unpleasantness of the assault.

But I don't want to be struck down elegantly!

The harsh, savage, joyous fire burning in Me Susane's breast became a furious blaze, fueled by sheer anger.

She struggled, kicked, tried to bite.

Her teeth briefly touched something soft and uncertain.

Meanwhile, he remained mute, stolid, almost accommodating, and it was beyond her to read his intentions.

Me Susane's fire only grew.

She clutched the arms that were holding her, scratched the bare, cold flesh, she might have cried out, might have sworn and cursed, she would never remember.

And then, shaken but silent, he loosened his grasp.

Launching her foot backward, she kicked him in the knee.

He stopped struggling with her, though he kept her clasped in his arms.

She sensed that he was limp and tender and somehow glad not to have triumphed.

Angrily, Me Susane whispered:

"Is that you, Principaux? Is that what your name is?"

He was still holding her.

All of a sudden she felt weak, his arms were stifling her.

She'd burned through her shame and cowardice, but also her boldness, self-possession, and nerve.

"What's your name?" she repeated, exhausted. "Principaux? Who are you to me?"

He let out a little laugh, but without cruelty or mockery.

"What about you?" he breathed.

He let her go, so unexpectedly that she almost fell to the

ground, even though she'd stayed on her feet all through the attack.

He ran off with a light, frivolous step.

"Principaux, I will never tell you who I am!" cried Me Susane. "Never, never, you hear?"

The taxi came along, and as Me Susane was getting in, still trembling, inflamed, and convinced that she'd won, she discovered her purse was gone.

When, a few days later, she was back in Bordeaux, the moment she'd been dreading turned out very differently from what she'd imagined.

Not only, when she had to tell Sharon her purse had been stolen and the marriage certificate with it, did Sharon seem neither shocked nor crushed, but Me Susane herself had a profound sense of an *unburdening*.

They were both standing in the kitchen, which Sharon had illuminated to the fullest.

Me Susane couldn't help putting her hand to her forehead.

Don't you see, Sharon, that my scar is as good as gone? Sharon, did you really not notice how terribly I was split open, how I was gouged?

It was still so cold in Bordeaux!

Drops of water trickled down the inside of the windows.

"What did he look like, this man who attacked you?" asked Sharon in a tone of polite curiosity.

They'd asked Me Susane the same question at the embassy, and all she could tell them, regretful but sincere and slightly uneasy, was:

"I don't know, I didn't see his face."

"Young? Middle-aged?"

"I couldn't tell you."

Similarly, she answered Sharon:

"I didn't see his face."

She sensed that Sharon wasn't unhappy to find the subject eliminated in this way.

"I'm so sorry," Me Susane began.

"It's not that important," Sharon interrupted.

"Yes, it is, for your file."

"I don't think so, no, don't worry about it."

Sharon was looking at Me Susane, puzzled and grave.

She said softly:

"Rudy's going to take my case off your hands, Madame Susane. He'll deal with it, that will be easier for you."

"Oh!" murmured Me Susane, at once shocked and immensely relieved.

"And also, Madame Susane . . ."

"Sharon, call me H . . ."

"And also, I'm going to stop working for you. It's not helpful, is it? My being here?"

Then, as was her habit, she abruptly walked out of the room.

That didn't mean, Me Susane was now allowing herself to think, that Sharon had some grievance against her, but only that, unable to understand her either in her motivations or in her aims, and feeling a regretful unease at that, she chose to relieve Me Susane of her presence, in case she might think that presence disapproving.

. . .

The next morning, Me Susane was vigorously striding toward her office when a delicate hand took her by the elbow.

A bitter wind whistled in the street.

The space between one place and another was nothing but grayness, drab sorrow.

But walking through that grimness did nothing to dampen Me Susane's high spirits, almost her euphoria, any more than Gilles Principaux's cautious fingers on her arm.

"I was just coming to see you," he said plaintively. "Where have you been? I came by your office so many times, and you were never in!"

"I'm back now," Me Susane said crisply.

"I see your limp is gone, that's good, I'm glad for you."

He tried to give her a friendly smile.

But his gaze remained at the same time tortured and vacant, caring nothing about what it had before it: Me Susane's face.

He didn't look well, his features were drawn, his hair scruffy about the ears.

You don't interest me and I'm not afraid of you anymore. You don't interest me, I've stopped trying to make out who you are to me. Now you're only Marlyne's husband, a certain Gilles Principaux, who I don't have to know anything about except what might prove useful for his wife's defense. You're undone, I fought and I won, you're no concern of mine anymore.

Since she'd spoken in silence, Principaux showed no reaction.

"Not only does Marlyne never want to see me again, she wants a divorce," he then said.

The cruel gusts of wind gave a touch of color to his long nose. Mᵉ Susane was shivering, but she didn't let it show.

He was standing there before her, Principaux—her client's husband, and nothing more.

Find the strength to resign yourself to that!

She studied his face, doing all she could to make herself unknown to him, to make the slightest of her features remind him of nothing at all.

In the office, Mᵉ Susane wrote her client who wanted to change his name.

She'd found a reference, buried parenthetically in a very old article on Bordeaux and the slave trade, to a certain person whose last name was not entirely unlike her client's—though two consonants and a vowel were different, which, Mᵉ Susane allowed herself to say in her email, was surely not enough to discount a family relationship between that person and her client.

No sooner had she sent off her message than the answer came back:

"Keep digging, Maître, keep digging, but above all, thank you! I already feel a connection to that N . . . , a repellent connection. A few letters' difference changes nothing, you know as well as I do that even within a family a name's spelling can vary. Thank you, Maître. I will never abandon my faith in the guilt of all the N . . . s in this city."

Then she received a woman from Bazas who, having struck one of her neighbors in the face and now finding herself the subject of a complaint, pressed Me Susane to support her in her conviction that there was nothing else she could have done.

Because every morning that neighbor, never picking up its excrement, allowed or even obliged his dog to defecate, deliberately, before the door of that woman who had endured this horridness for many long years.

"Maître, I snapped, isn't that normal? I punched him in the nose, in his horrible sneering nose. My fingers still hurt. But what could I do?"

One cold, dark Sunday noontime, Me Susane was sitting in her parents' kitchen, on her usual chair.

She felt at the same time moved and bewildered, as if it were some astonishing stroke of fate that had brought her to her childhood home, not her will or desire, she could scarcely even picture herself driving her ancient Twingo to La Réole—oh, how dour and disdainful was the old city in the grips of winter!

Rudy and Lila, who'd arrived before her, settled into their customary places, plied Madame Susane with coaxing displays of hungry impatience for the first course, an assortment of pâtés and sausages.

Madame Susane was exceptionally dressed up, genial, almost frolicsome.

In her ears she wore the discreet pearls from her days as a fiancée.

And her short, sparse hair had been freshly dyed, thought Me Susane, a chestnut-red color that she didn't recall ever seeing on her mother before, and which, when Madame Susane opened the door to her, had left her speechless: Who on earth is this woman?

Madame Susane suddenly lifted her hands over her cutting board.

She slowly moved them away from her breast, opened her slightly trembling fingers like blooming flowers.

"My daughter, I'm so happy you're here," she whispered.

Her eyes began to glisten.

Monsieur Susane, standing beside her, leaned with both hands on the back of a chair.

Moved, he sucked at his lower lip even as he cast glances at Me Susane seeking forgiveness for this display of emotion.

"We're all very happy, yes!" exclaimed Rudy.

He leapt to his feet, gave Madame Susane a hug.

Then he bent down and threw his arms around Me Susane's shoulders.

"Doing OK, little mama?" he murmured in her ear.

Such was his customary nickname for her, teasing and affectionate, when they were a couple.

But how dumbstruck Me Susane had been when she followed the chestnut-haired woman into the kitchen and she found Rudy and Lila there!

Rudy had kissed her on the lips.

Lila had pressed herself to her breast, whimpering with pleasure.

What hell are we emerging from? Me Susane had wondered, bewildered.

What battle?

And did we win?

Who are we, in this place, to each other?

Who is Lila to me?

A wound, a sign, a stroke of good fortune?

A Mystery?

She feverishly searched the little girl's face while Rudy, as he always had—by which means he'd earned, sweetly, openly, with no taint of condescension, the Susanes' deathless devotion—joked with his hosts.

"I'm not going to get my beach body back with you two around," he pretended to grumble, comically sniffing at the rich, fatty smells streaming from the oven.

"You need to put some flesh on your bones, my poor fellow!" objected Monsieur Susane.

"It's true, you're horribly thin."

Madame Susane pinched Rudy's flat, hard, athletic stomach, took the liberty of pulling up his shirt to touch, as loving mothers or mothers-in-law do, or smitten wives or girlfriends, his warm, innocent flesh.

That little kitchen was suffused with a wholesome joy, Me Susane told herself in astonishment.

Lila looked up at her, her features cleansed of all desolation.

She was open and neutral, content—too much so? Me Susane asked herself.

The memory of no torment, no daze, no lie could be glimpsed on her apparently confident face.

Me Susane stroked her neck, behind her ears.

Lila purred.

But did her enigmatic expectations, her impenetrable wishes, not require that she seem perfectly, outrageously at peace?

And, Me Susane asked herself with a certain terror, wasn't it the case that Lila, not wanting to be a bother to Rudy, had fallen into the habit of continually displaying all the outward signs of serenity?

She put her hands on Lila's cheeks.

The child's face was opaque, mute, impermeable to any hope of understanding.

But Me Susane didn't want to spoil the warm, happy atmosphere delimited and ennobled by the white light of the opaline ceiling lamp, wanted it so little that she didn't even try to hold back Madame Susane's hand as she served Lila seconds of every dish: charcuterie, leg of lamb, potatoes dauphine, ice-cream cones.

Why are you stuffing her like that? Don't you see she has a weight problem?

She said nothing, smiling and, all things considered, more or less happy.

Whenever her eyes met Lila's her lips silently formed these words: I've come back.

Deep in her lonely heart Lila understood her, perhaps.

After the coffee, as the Susanes were taking Lila into their daughter's old bedroom for her nap, Rudy pulled his chair close to Me Susane's.

Laying his light, delicate hands on her shoulders, he softly said:

"We love her so, you and I."

Madame Judge, Mesdames and Messieurs of the Jury . . .

. . . For what do we know of what happened in that house, and what do we know of the sorrows, the fears and hatreds, the disgusts, the resentments whose memory it preserves? The house knows everything and forgets nothing. Put to torture by our ruthless minds, it does not always stand silent. Let us make it speak, that pretty house in Le Bouscat where Marlyne, Gilles, Jason, John, and Julia supposedly led a quiet life, conventionally happy, banally devoted to the perpetuation of ever-unspoken antagonisms . . .

. . . What happened in that house? Enormous wings enfolded it, darkness fell over it . . .

. . . Gilles Principaux uses the darkness, he feeds his obsession, works on his plan: that Marlyne be surrounded by solitude . . .

. . . That he become the only adult in Marlyne's circle . . .

. . . The children don't matter, and their nice papa fills them with terror . . .

... A furious, unjust god, his decisions unpredictable but irreversible ...

... The children matter only with respect to that one pre-occupation: creating an emptiness around Marlyne ...

... She must be not only sequestered but confined, locked away of her own accord ...

... No, to Gilles Principaux the children are of no importance. Nor do they matter to that complicitous house, the house that sees all and never tells, the house that loves no one but prefers to ally itself with whoever has the most power within its walls ... Yes, houses are cowards, the walls hold their tongues. And yet, sometimes, we can force them to testify ...

... Who is he, then, this Principaux with his many names, this dark angel of the hearth?

... Today the house confesses ...

... Yes, Mesdames and Messieurs of the Jury, the house confesses, the house that collaborates in the crime, it confesses, it says: I was that man's accomplice ...

... Who is he, then? We think we know now, but still we wonder: Could I be mistaken?

Marie NDiaye was born in Pithiviers, France, and studied linguistics at the Sorbonne. She is the author of *Rosie Carpe,* winner of the Prix Femina, and of *Three Strong Women,* winner of the Prix Goncourt. She is also the recipient of the Gold Medal in the Arts from the Kennedy Center International Committee on the Arts. She lives in Paris.

A NOTE ON THE TYPE

This book was set in Hoefler Text, a family of fonts
created by Jonathan Hoefler, who was born in 1970.
First designed in 1991, Hoefler Text was intended as an
advancement on existing desktop computer typography,
including as it does an exponentially larger number of
glyphs than previous fonts. In form, Hoefler Text looks
to the old-style fonts of the seventeenth century, but it is
wholly of its time, employing a precision and sophistica-
tion only available to the late twentieth century.

Composed by Berryville Graphics,
Berryville, Virginia

Printed and bound by Berryville Graphics,
Berryville, Virginia

Book design by Pei Loi Koay